"Need me

Cooper walked out the back room like he owned the place.

Lainey hated that she noticed his body. That she wanted to run her fingers across the muscles she'd pretended not to notice.

Because that way lay madness.

That way lay hockey.

"What's your game here, Slick?"

"What the hell do you want me to say?"

His genuine surprise pissed her off more. Because she'd promised herself she was done with hockey. With hockey players.

She pulled him down until their mouths were practically touching.

"I don't want you to say anything." Lainey caught Cooper's bottom lip between her teeth. Oh, God, he felt good. Big. Strong. Like he could handle what she was dishing out tonight.

She wanted sex. She wanted to punish him for making her feel this way. For making her want things she couldn't have.

Dear Reader,

Well, it's the end of an era. My last Harlequin Blaze. And I can't think of a better book to cap off my hat trick.

As a former hockey player, I always knew I wanted to write a hockey-playing heroine, and Lainey was the perfect mix of heart and grit to keep Cooper in line, on the ice and in the bedroom...and the bar... and the parking garage. *wink*

My time with Blaze has been a dream come true from start to finish, and I've gotten to work with so many talented people along the way. From cover art to copy edits to moral support, every single person who has touched my books has made them better, and I thank them for that.

And I thank you, too. For taking a chance on a new author, and for choosing to spend your valuable time and resources on the stories I tell. You're the best. The absolute best. I couldn't do this without you.

To show my appreciation, I present to you a tale of snarky banter and sexy times.

And don't be a stranger, okay? When you're done reading, come find me inside your computer or smartphone at tarynleightaylor.com, Facebook.com/ tarynltaylor1 and @tarynltaylor. We can be cyber BFFs.

Keep on dreaming out loud,

Taryn Leigh Taylor

Taryn Leigh Taylor

Playing Dirty

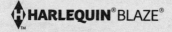

Recycling programs
for this product may
not exist in your area.

ISBN-13: 978-0-373-79966-4

Playing Dirty

Copyright © 2017 by Taryn Leigh Taylor

Printed in U.S.A.

Taryn Leigh Taylor likes dinosaurs, bridges and space, both personal and of the final-frontier variety. She shamelessly indulges in clichés, most notably her Starbucks addiction (grande six-pump whole-milk no-water chai-tea latte, aka: the usual), her shoe hoard (*I can stop anytime I... Ooh! These are pretty!*) and her penchant for falling in lust with fictional men with great abs. She also really loves books, which was what sent her down the crazy path of writing one in the first place.

Want to be virtual friends? Check out tarynleightaylor.com, Facebook.com/tarynleightaylor1 and Twitter, @tarynltaylor.

Books by Taryn Leigh Taylor

Harlequin Blaze

Kiss and Makeup
Playing to Win

To get the inside scoop on Harlequin Blaze and its talented writers, but sure to check out Facebook.com/BlazeAuthors.

All backlist available in ebook format.

Visit the Author Profile page at Harlequin.com.

Fay—Thank you for your opinion. (I know it's funnier if I leave it at that, but honestly, I couldn't do what I do without your help. If I could sum you up in emoji form, you'd be all four thumbs up *and* the winky face. And you know that's the highest praise I can bestow.)

Liz—Writing this book without you would be like seeing Mulder sans hideous tie—unthinkable. (Unless he's wearing a Speedo.)

This book is for Jenn, Neil, Brad, Lora and Yvette, Craig and Leila—y'all cheer for the wrong hockey teams, but your friendship and support mean the world.

1

"IT'S ABOUT DAMN time you got here, Darius. I know my fa—I know Martin wasn't much for punctuality, but if you want to keep working here, you're going to have to show up on time."

Lainey kicked the beer fridge closed and froze, as though the act had triggered a curse that turned her to stone. In truth, though, her paralysis was directly attributable to the animal magnetism of the man on the other side of the counter.

Black hair just long enough to curl against his collar? Check.

Dark stubble framing a smirking mouth? Check.

Muscled arms that could make angels weep and women purr?

Check and check.

"You're…" Cooper Mead, number sixteen, the Portland Storm's latest acquisition, currently tied for highest scoring defenseman in the league. "Not Darius."

"Nope." The single syllable, deep and rough, was enough to detonate an estrogen grenade low in her tummy.

Dammit.

Cooper freakin' Mead! Standing in Martin's crappy little sports bar—*her* crappy little sports bar now, she reminded herself. And boy, was he something to behold. All six feet two inches and 220 pounds of him, per the team stats page. Lainey cursed the lapse in internet browsing judgment that had led to that knowledge. She hadn't watched hockey, talked hockey, *thought* of hockey in years, but in the three months since she'd come back to Portland, the nadir of all her broken dreams and bad luck, she was already falling into bad habits.

And Cooper Mead was the kind of bad habit that would be hard to break.

With great effort, Lainey beat back the hormonal fallout and cast a wary glance around the bar. Oregon might be a long way from Denmark, but something here was definitely rotten.

The Drunken Sportsman wasn't the type of place that attracted professional athletes. Hell, some weeks it barely attracted enough armchair athletes to keep the lights on and the doors open.

Right now, there were two groups of them, a middle-aged couple sporting his and hers Trail Blazers T-shirts and eating nachos in the booth farthest from the door, and four guys at a table by the window who were stretching a pitcher of beer as far as it could go while staring zombie-like at the basketball pregame coverage on the hulking television above the bar.

She needed to replace it with a couple of flat screens spread around the room for more optimal viewing. She made a mental note to add that to her list and turned back to the defensive juggernaut who stood across from her.

Other than him, there was nothing—and no one—out

of place. And yet something about the situation had her on edge. She glanced at Cooper Mead's wicked mouth, the corner quirked up in a grin that did weird things to her insides.

Maybe I'm allergic to hockey.

Squaring her shoulders, Lainey strove for professionalism in the form of the official bartender's mantra. "So, not-Darius, what'll it be?"

"How about Sex on the Beach and a Screaming Orgasm?"

No.

Don't say it, she thought with a desperation that surprised her. *Please don't go there.*

A flicker of indecision crossed his handsome face, one that gave her hope that her telepathy had worked. Then he turned on that easy grin, bracing an arm on the bar and leaning closer.

"But if I'm going to do my best work," he confided in a soft growl that prickled between her shoulder blades, "I'll probably need something to drink first."

Aaaand he went there.

"Good one. Very original. You'd think, with me being a bartender and all, I would've heard that one before." She forced herself not to roll her eyes. If getting hit on in bars had taught her anything, it was that derision had more impact when delivered with some restraint. It was important not to cross into "the lady doth protest too much" territory or the playboys and the drunks would never leave you alone.

In response, he upped the wattage of his smile and reached over the bar to liberate a maraschino cherry from the fruit caddy.

"Sarcasm. Nice. You're feisty. I like that." He popped

the pointedly sexual fruit in his mouth and chewed. "But in my defense, it's not the small-talk portion of the evening I excel at. Give me your number and I'll prove it to you."

Lainey wanted to be offended, she really did, but damned if his megalomania wasn't working for him, in a basic "the hormones want what the hormones want" kind of way. Still, a woman had to have standards.

"Listen, I appreciate the display of manly bravado, but as much as I'd like to stand here and fend off your advances, I've got a drink quota to maintain. You actually want something, or are you just here to waste my time?" Lainey crossed her arms over her white tank top. Cooper Mead wasn't the only talented defenseman here. Her nickname hadn't been "The Ice Queen" for nothing.

The memory came out of nowhere, like a slap shot to her brain—fast, powerful, and it hurt like a bitch. Her pulse thundered in her right wrist, the one she'd busted in the last hockey game she'd ever played, and she shook her hand to dislodge the sensation. No one had referred to her by her old hockey nickname in ages. The fact that she'd been the one to break that streak said a lot.

One more reason she couldn't let her guard down. She needed to fix up the bar, sell it for a tidy profit and get the hell out of Portland back to the fabulous, hockey-less life she'd built for herself. The sooner, the better.

It had taken hard work and single-minded focus to become one of the Zenith Advisory Group's top hospitality consultants. And sure, that was just a fancy way of saying that she traveled the country staying in nice hotels and filling out comment cards—but the title came with a generous wage and her choice of locations. Which was why she'd never taken an assignment in Portland before.

Too many ghosts here, and all of them wore skates.

Cooper shot a pointed glance around the almost-deserted bar. "What happens if you don't make the drink quota?" He twirled the cherry stem absently between his finger and thumb. He had big hands.

"Oh, you know, swarm of locusts, rain of fire, four guys on horseback."

He nodded, flicking the stem aside. "And what if I guarantee to make any trouble worth your while?"

She didn't like the way her heart sped up at the vow or the way she believed that he could make good on it. "Nice try, Slick, but I wasn't kidding about the drink quota, so you're gonna have to tell me what you want."

Cooper propped an elbow on the bar. "And here I thought I'd been pretty clear about what I want."

"To drink. What do you want to drink?"

"Surprise me."

With a cocked eyebrow, she grabbed a highball glass and turned toward the liquor bottles that lined the shelves. Lainey couldn't help but steal glances at him in the mirrored tiles that stretched from counter to ceiling behind the booze. Damned if she wasn't kind of impressed that a guy who would approach with the lamest of lame pickup lines wasn't standing there ogling her ass. He lifted a hand to rub the back of his neck as he waited, and Lainey noticed for the first time that he looked tired—not like he needed a nap, but like it would be nice to put down the weight of the world for a little while.

She knew *exactly* how he felt.

"Here's your drink."

She turned to face him and set it on the counter. Despite her earlier pang of empathy, she took great pleasure in the distrustful frown that had overtaken his rugged features.

"Are you sure you didn't grab the wrong glass? Because, and trust me here, I've had some experience ordering drinks and they usually come in liquid form."

Lainey had to admit the congealed glob that came from mixing Bailey's and Sour Puss looked particularly disgusting tonight. The fact that it was floating in Kahlua and Blue Curacao added a previously unsurpassed level of yuck. She lifted one bare shoulder in an offhand shrug. "You're the one who wanted a surprise."

"Yes, I was."

"I call it a Black Widow."

"Of course you do," he said, but she had a feeling the mockery was self-directed. "How much?"

"Twenty."

Straight black brows flicked upward. "As in 'US dollars'?"

"Ten for the drink and the rest is the standard first-time penalty for pickup lines that insult my intelligence."

Cooper's lips twitched with reluctant humor. "Well, just so long as it's not to cover the going rate for arsenic."

"You never know," she warned, nudging the Black Widow toward him with the tip of her red-polished fingernail. "You feelin' lucky, Slick?"

He smiled for real then, a full-fledged, blindingly white smile that kept some dentist's classic Corvette on the road. "I wouldn't mind getting lucky."

Lainey shook off a flash of reignited lust. *Damn, he was good.* "Well, the night is young. Maybe your left hand hasn't made plans yet."

She forced herself not to flinch at the blunder. It was a fatal error to let an egocentric hockey player know you knew anything about him—especially fangirl minutia, like the fact that Cooper Mead was a southpaw.

"Oooooh. So it's gonna be like that, huh? I thought you weren't supposed to start eating me alive until *after* the sex."

She ignored the black widow reference and held out an expectant hand.

With a self-deprecating nod, Cooper dug out his wallet and handed her a fifty. Her palm tingled where his skin brushed hers. "Would I be wrong to assume you're fresh out of change?" He didn't wait for confirmation before stowing the billfold away.

Lainey tucked Ulysses S. Grant safely into her back pocket. Leaning forward, she rested her elbows on the counter. "You know, you're a much smarter man than first impressions would indicate."

"You like 'em brainy, huh?" He mimicked her position, cutting the gap between them. His eyes were dark, like rich espresso, and just as heart-pounding as a jolt of caffeine. The kind of eyes a girl could get lost in if she wasn't careful.

Lucky for her, Lainey was always careful.

"Personally, I find the brain usually gets in the way of all the exciting stuff, but I completely respect alternate lifestyle choices," Cooper continued. "We should hang out sometime. You can help me see the error of my ways. Give me your number and we'll make this happen."

He reached out and tucked a wayward strand of raven hair behind her ear. When his knuckles brushed her cheek, her knees went squishy. And that was *before* he whispered, "Don't break my heart, gorgeous. Give me your number."

"Wow." Lainey pushed back from the bar, unwillingly

impressed and a little woozy from the flare of attraction. "Wow. That was…masterful. Seriously, Slick. You are very, very good."

His slow, self-mocking grin confirmed that the jig was up. "I almost had you at the end there."

"Not even close," she lied.

"Sure I was. But you were a worthy opponent. It's been a long time since someone gave me a run for my money, and considering the number at the bottom of my last bank statement, that's saying something."

Since the Storm had signed him to a two-year, eight-million-dollar contract, she knew his boasting was legit. "Is this the part where I'm supposed to be impressed?"

"It would help," he agreed, down but not out. "I'll give you five hundred bucks for your number."

"Forget it."

"A thousand."

Lainey bit back a grin. "If you'll excuse me, I have a bar to run."

"Fifteen hundred. Final offer."

It was tempting. Not the money, the man himself. She'd been working nonstop for the last few months to put her affairs in order in Portland. And once he'd gotten his dismal approach out of the way, their verbal sparring had been kind of fun.

But she needed to stay far away from hockey—and even farther away from famous men. She'd be better off if Cooper Mead walked out of her bar and just kept walking, no matter what her long-suffering libido had to say on the matter.

"Enjoy your night, Slick. Thanks for the dance." And with that, she shoved a sign that read WAITSTAFF ONLY on the counter and turned her back on him, more determined than ever to unload the bar and blend back into the familiar hustle and bustle of LA by the end of the month.

HE WAS GETTING too damn old for this.

Coop grabbed his glass from the counter. Revulsion curled his lip as he stared at the sludge he'd just been served while the dust from his spectacular crash and burn settled around him. A post-practice night out with his teammates used to mean a luxurious night in the VIP room of some exclusive New York club, complete with overpriced bottle service, an overhyped DJ and an underdressed woman. Or two.

Since he'd taken the trade to Portland, there'd been a couple of team dinners, a little charity work and a whole lot of practices. But that's how the Storm had all but guaranteed their spot in the postseason over a month ago. Intense focus.

In fact, it had been so much all-work-and-no-play that his agent, Jared Golden, had called to give Cooper hell. "I can't get endorsement deals for a hermit, Mead. Leaving New York is already hurting your visibility. You know how much harder it is for me to get your picture in a magazine when you're in Portland? At least go out and live a little."

Which was why Cooper had finally relented and accepted one of fellow defenseman Brett Sillinger's relentless requests to "grab a beer and talk hockey." He fully regretted the decision now.

He'd assumed there would be a group of them heading out for one last drink before playoffs got underway. But when he'd asked around the dressing room after practice, it turned out he was on his own. Every player on the team had somewhere else to be—captain Luke Maguire was going to some media shindig with his intrepid reporter girlfriend, centerman Eric Jacobs was meeting some after-hours contractor at the bakery he owned and goaltender Tyson Mackinaw's kids were performing in some school play.

The rest of the team's excuses followed in those footsteps: wife, wife, girlfriend, kids, girlfriend's kids.

Jesus. Everyone on this damn team was—or acted like—an old married guy.

Except for him…and Brett of course.

And for reasons Cooper couldn't possibly explain, the rookie had chosen the worst bar imaginable—a rundown watering hole that probably catered to former high school jocks bent on reliving their glory days through ESPN highlights. And he didn't even have the decency to show up on time.

As if to confirm Cooper's suspicions, the bell on the door dinged and in lumbered a whole flock of washed-up jocks decked out in the finest basketball paraphernalia the mall had to offer.

"Hey there, beautiful lady. Turn up that TV! The game starts in ten minutes."

Coop's fingers tightened on his Black Widow. The bartender's smile was full-bodied and sexy when it wasn't tinged with acid, and he hated that some loudmouth sporting love handles and an ill-fitting Trail Blazers jersey was the recipient and not him.

"Larry, you only think I'm beautiful because I didn't raise the happy hour price of beer." Her admonishment was accompanied by the familiar singsong lilt of sportscasters everywhere as she hit the volume button on the remote.

"Sweetcheeks—" Cooper did his best to stifle a gag at the endearment "—you know that's not true. One word from you and I'd—holy hockey pucks, you're Cooper Mead!"

So much for lying low.

"Wow, you're, like, a real athlete! A famous one! Man, you think you could sign something for my kid? He totally idolizes you! And the guys! The whole team! I do, too. I mean, that slap shot of yours? Big fan. We all are! Thanks to you, the Storm might have a real shot in the playoffs." He offered with an expansive gesture. "Guys! Check it out! Cooper Mead! At our bar."

The chorus of greetings and swears of disbelief were accompanied by the materialization of cell phones. Calls were placed. Photos were snapped. The couple from the other side of the bar wandered over. Not exactly how he'd planned to spend his evening, but at least Golden would be happy.

With a resigned sigh, he brought his drink to his lips.

He stopped just in time.

Suicide by toxic sludge was never the answer.

Instead, Cooper turned on his best PR smile and accepted the napkin being thrust in his direction. "Who should I make this out to?"

"What the hell happened here?"

The deep voice ripped into a close inspection of her palm, and Lainey looked up from her crouched position in front of the open beer fridge. From this vantage point, the man fingering the assortment of bottles she'd left on the counter appeared even taller than usual.

Darius Johnson. Prelaw student, smart-ass and not a

big fan of hers. Which Lainey figured made sense, see-ing as he was her fa—*Martin's* last hire.

Also, she'd cleaned house when she'd first arrived, fir-ing a dishonest bartender and a couple of slothful wait-resses. Despite the months that had passed, Lainey got the impression that the remaining staff were still a little wary that she'd go all "off with their heads" on them at any moment. She didn't bother doing anything to dis-abuse them of that notion. It didn't matter if Darius was fun to spar with, or that she kind of enjoyed Aggie's no-nonsense wisdom. Lainey was here to sell the bar. She wasn't looking to make friends.

All in all, Darius was a solid bartender and great with the regulars. And Lainey wasn't above exploiting the fact that he was popular with the coeds—they loved his soul-ful eyes, café-au-lait complexion and killer smile. Or at least those were some of the giggled compliments she'd heard when they were gathered at the counter, fawning over him on a Friday night. They didn't seem to mind his stupid goatee, either.

She let the flirting stand, because if you could get the ladies into a bar, the guys would follow. And the fact that some of Darius's fellow students were choosing to spend their money in a crappy sports bar instead of a flashy nightclub did good things for the bottom line. And it was a bottom line that needed all the help it could get.

Still, that didn't keep her from imagining firing Dar-ius at least three times per shift, if only for the peace and quiet.

"Give me a hard time for not keeping my workspace clear, but I show up to a mess of bottles on the counter when you're in charge," he muttered, the way he always did when he was trying to get under her skin.

"It was recipe development," she said simply. "It's called a Black Widow."

Darius frowned as he set the Cinnamon Schnapps back on the shelf. "You put all this stuff in the same glass? Whoever he was, he must've really pissed you off."

Embarrassed, Lainey rubbed her fingers against her cheek in a vain attempt to extinguish the lingering prickle where Cooper's knuckles had touched her. "Don't think I didn't notice that you're late." She made sure her voice was as frosty as the draft mugs that rattled when she slammed the cooler door. "For future reference, your shifts are posted in Pacific Time."

Darius glanced over his shoulder as he returned the Kahlua, the Blue Curacao and some banana liqueur to the appropriate shelves. "He definitely pissed you off."

"*You* pissed me off," Lainey corrected, standing. "I know Martin let stuff like this slide, but I'm trying to sell this place. I can't afford not to have things running smoothly."

"You keep saying that, but you've been here for three months and counting. I'm starting to think we're never gonna be rid of you."

Lainey pulled a face at his broad back when he turned to clean up her mess.

"You know I can see you in this mirror, right?"

She schooled her features into a neutral expression. "And you know that I have the power to fire you, right?"

"Well, before you let all your authority go to your head and I end up suing you for wrongful termination, you should probably check your phone. I texted you that I was running late. But I'll let it go, because I'm in a stellar mood. Sandra and I shared a hell of a goodbye before her Uber showed up to take her to the airport."

Darius's expression was dripping with satisfaction. "Which is why I got here late, if you know what I mean." He waited a beat. "And what I mean is that we had copious amounts of sexual intercourse."

"Thanks for the clarification, wonder stud." Lainey rolled her eyes at him. "But I'm not sure that's the type of excuse that will stand up in court. As a future lawyer, you'll want to familiarize yourself with labor laws."

The well-timed entrance of Agnes Demille saved Lainey from Darius's retort. The zaftig waitress materialized from the "Staff Only" door to their right, plopped her massive gold lamé purse on the counter behind the bar, grimaced and slung it back on her shoulder. "Honestly, you two. I've been here for thirty seconds, and there's already a table full of customers with no beer and a sticky counter. This ain't no way to run a business. 'Specially on game night. Let's get a move on, people! Darius, hand me that rag."

Darius peeled the blue rag from the sink and dropped it in front of Aggie, who set to work immediately, scrubbing at the sticky rings on the counter. "So, Lainey," she said, not bothering to look up from her task, "I'm thinkin' the two of us need to have a little chitchat."

Lainey ignored the resulting shiver down her spine. Aggie could size up a room quicker than anyone Lainey had ever met, and she didn't miss a detail. Especially not a ridiculously handsome one wielding a glass full of sludge. In an attempt to sidestep the conversation, Lainey placed a tray on the counter and systematically loaded it with six frosty bottles of beer from the cooler. "Beers for Larry's table, as requested."

Unfortunately, the announcement didn't faze the formidable woman before her. "They can wait. What you just did to Cooper Mead can't."

"What?" Darius's brows dove into a V as he scanned the customers. A sharp bark of laughter confirmed he'd located his target. "Are you kidding me? The Black Widow was for Cooper Mead? That is so awesome!" He held up an expectant palm in her direction, then thought better of it and aborted the high five. "Man, it sucks I was late! I would've loved to have seen his face when you handed it over. So what's Mr. Big Shot doing here, anyway?"

"Bible study starts in ten minutes."

Darius shot Lainey a pained smile as she bent to grab a bottle of water from the fridge.

"Well, don't be a moron. It's a bar, for God's sake. What do you think he's doing here?"

"It's a floundering sports bar," he corrected pointedly. "Hardly the preferred scene of professional athletes."

Lainey stiffened at the comment. "Then you should be glad he's here. He shelled out for his drink, so you might actually get paid on time this week."

Darius had the grace to blush. "You know I didn't mean it like that."

"Yeah, I know." Twisting open her water, Lainey took a long swallow and stared blankly at a framed hockey jersey—number 42—on the opposite wall. "I have no idea what he's doing here, either," she confessed.

Lainey took another bracing gulp of water, screwed the lid back on and turned to meet Aggie's unrelenting stare.

"It's no big deal," Lainey assured the carroty-hued waitress. Further proof that cheap self-tanning lotion, like Cooper Mead, was one more on a long list of items to be avoided.

"He fed me a lame line, I gave him a disgusting drink. As you can see, he didn't take it too hard." She gestured toward a smiling Cooper as he posed for a camera phone.

"Just because a man notices you got a nice rack don't mean you need to start handin' out the Black Widows." Agnes shook her frizzy, brassy-hued curls. "I never shoulda told you about those."

"She's right, Lainey," Darius interjected. "You do have a nice rack."

She landed a hard punch on his shoulder. "Back off, pervert."

Lainey turned back to Aggie with "I told you so" plastered all over her expression. "You see? I'm rude to all overbearing jackasses! It's what I do."

Agnes planted a fist on one generous, black-spandex-covered hip. "Yeah, but Cooper Mead ain't every other jackass."

"Oh, no? And what makes him so special?"

"That's what I'd like to know," Darius threw in.

"I mean, sure, he's gorgeous," Lainey conceded. "And there's no denying the way that voice rumbles through your chest and trickles down to all the right places, and yeah, okay, I may have almost had an orgasm just looking at him."

Aggie nodded dreamily, and both women shot a wistful look in Cooper's direction. Not that they were bonding or anything. This was strictly physical appreciation of a handsome man, not friendship.

"I can't believe Cooper Mead is signing beer coasters in your sports bar!" Aggie sighed. "It's like a freakin' fairy tale or somethin'."

"Funny. I don't actually remember the part in *Cinderella* when she had to change her panties."

Lainey grimaced, disgusted out of her aesthetic appreciation. "Ugh. Darius. Seriously. Why do you have to be such a guy?"

"You do realize you're practically forcing me to grab my crotch right now, don't you?"

"All I'm sayin'," Aggie stressed, "is that sometimes you gotta swallow your pride, think of the big picture. Normally when you castrate someone, the fate of your business ain't riding on it."

"What?" Lainey rolled her eyes. "The fate of my business is hardly riding on Cooper Mead's penis."

Darius's snicker earned him two glares. "What? You said *penis*."

"It's resting on my shoulders," Lainey countered, with the pious look of stone angels the world over. "And I can handle it."

"I know you can! But use that big ol' brain of yours. Bein' attentive to a man with fame and money is just good business sense."

Lainey turned her head to hide her frown.

"Cooper Mead is the Pied Piper of cool an' you darn well know it. Where he goes, the puck bunnies and the sports fans follow. I don't think makin' nice with him is too much to ask! You know, most joints would kill to have a pro athlete walk through their door! And you're the one always jabbering about selling this joint."

"You do realize that Mr. Rich and Famous over there was interested in my phone number, not an endorsement deal," Lainey pointed out.

"I think you mean Mr. Sexy, Rich and Famous." Agnes sent an appreciative glance at the object of their discussion, who appeared to be talking to someone's kid via FaceTime. "Emphasis on the sexy."

"Well, Mr. *Sexy*, Rich and Famous," Lainey amended, "is kind of a shallow, conceited jerk, emphasis on the jerk."

"Who cares? I don't wanna waste time talkin' to him! Man who looks that good could have me anytime, anywhere."

Heat, not unlike the sear of a good shot of whisky, burned in Lainey's stomach at the thought of Cooper and sex, and her mind was seized by an alarmingly vivid vision of him, naked on a king-size battlefield, expertly wielding his…uh, sword.

Luckily the flashing of a disturbingly high number on the "Now Serving" sign above the imaginary bed doused the flame before it reddened her cheeks.

"Listen, your daddy was a good guy, but a so-so businessman. This place can use all the good publicity it can get. 'Specially the free kind." Oblivious to Lainey's inner turmoil, Agnes walked to the other side of the counter and hefted the tray of beer to her shoulder. "I'm gonna deliver these, but I want you to promise me that when you turn around and see that a certain teammate of his is here, you're going to play nice, okay? Take care of things nice and quiet. Don't make a scene."

Aggie's warning tone left little doubt as to the identity of Cooper's teammate, and Lainey's gaze jerked to the newly occupied table in the back corner, near the stage.

With a curse, she stomped out from behind the bar with every intent of telling table seventeen to go to hell, despite Aggie's well-meaning advice.

2

WHEN COOPER HAD finished smiling for the camera, he found Brett smirking at him from a table at the back of the bar.

Perfect timing.

Cooper wasn't exactly sure what he'd done to piss off Fate, but she sure knew how to hold a grudge. With a deep, steadying breath, he straightened his shoulders, braced for sniper fire and marched manfully to the seat Brett had saved for him.

Cooper placed his drink on the table and flopped into the empty chair.

Sillinger leaned indolently back in his own, his ball cap pulled witness-protection-program low to avoid the autograph gauntlet that Coop had just endured. "So? How'd it go, Romeo? Did you use the drink pickup line? Did she bite?"

Cooper bit back the expletives he wished he could unleash, and, with a disgusted shake of his head, reached into his wallet and shoved a pile of crisp fifties at his teammate. It was his own damn fault. He never should have made the bet in the first place. But sometimes when the kid wouldn't stop yammering, it was easier to give in than listen to him talk.

Brett smiled and gathered the cash. Cooper leaned forward and folded his arms on the table, a move that brought him eye-level with the thick, muddy mixture in his glass. He couldn't remember seeing many things more unappetizing than the tar-like substance. But if he was being honest, he'd had a pretty good time ordering it. It had been way too long since he'd indulged in flirtatious banter, and the hot bartender was an accomplished adversary.

"That drink looks like it tastes like shit. What is it?"

"This," he said as dismissively as he could manage, straightening in his chair, "is a Black Widow."

Sillinger's choked laughter was right on cue, but it made Cooper's hands tighten into fists anyway.

It was an old habit, one he'd picked up on the playground back when teasing often escalated to getting knocked around. With a purposeful breath, Cooper unclenched his fingers.

"A Black Widow?"

"Yep."

"But isn't that the spider that—"

Cooper hid his grimace beneath disdain. "Yep."

The little punk howled with laughter. "That's fuckin' classic! She shut you down hard!"

Annoyed, Cooper shoved the evidence of his earlier defeat aside with enough force to send some of the mud-colored goo oozing over the rim. He should have ignored his agent and ditched Brett, and just gone home after practice.

He wasn't in Portland to make friends, he reminded himself. He was here to make sure his hockey legacy included a championship ring, not just a bunch of tabloid stories.

"You know what, Sillinger? Why don't you…"

He trailed off, immediately and viscerally aware that the instigator of this gong show was making her way toward his table, and while he was enjoying the way her wavy black hair flirted with the tops of her breasts, her determined stride and laser-eyes made it clear this was not going to be pleasant encounter. He braced for impact as she drew near.

"Get out."

Anger surged, but before he could open his mouth, Sillinger was already beaking.

"And the Ice Queen strikes again. Nice to see you too, sis."

Well, shit. He hadn't seen that one coming.

"I'm serious, Brett. Leave."

Cooper relaxed in his chair at the interesting turn of events.

"C'mon, Elaine. Be cool. I'm here with my teammate." He raised his eyebrows pleadingly.

"I told you, I go by Lainey now," she ground out. "And when you turn twenty-one, that reason will hold water. Now get out."

When her gaze remained steely, the rookie's voice broke into a whine. "Other bars let me in. I've got ID."

Her mouth fell open as he pulled his license from his wallet and held it in her direction.

Lainey reached across the table and snatched it from his fingers. "Did you honestly just show me a fake ID? What the hell is wrong with you?" She took a step to the left and Sillinger bolted out of his chair and did the same, maintaining the distance between them.

"Dad used to let me hang out!"

"I'm sure that will look great on his posthumous father-of-the-year trophy." Lainey feinted left again, but dodged right. Brett didn't fall for the fake out.

"Honestly, Brett, I don't have time for your bullshit. Now get your nineteen-year-old ass the hell out of my bar, before I make you." Sillinger might have a couple inches and sixty-five pounds on her, but Coop's money was on her if it came to blows.

Brett heaved a put-upon sigh. "All you do is bitch about how desperate you are for customers, and when I bring you some, you kick us out?"

"I'm kicking *you* out. Your teammate is welcome to stay."

"Funny, that's not quite the impression I got earlier," Coop interjected.

She spared him a dismissive frown before turning her attention back to her brother. Brett's glare deepened as they faced off from across the table. Lainey stayed cool, raising an eyebrow and crossing her arms. Cooper wasn't surprised when the kid caved first.

"Fine. You just lost our business. Hope you're happy."

Brett's voice cracked a little as he threw down the ultimatum, and despite the posturing, it was obvious the kid was desperately afraid Coop wouldn't follow his lead.

Truth be told, Cooper felt for him. It was an eternity ago now, but he'd been the same in his youth—cocky as hell, with more money than brains and a desperate need to be accepted by the team.

Brett's gaze turned imploring. "You coming?"

The tough-guy ambivalence was ruined by the quaver in his voice.

"Give me a minute. I'll be right out."

The kid glanced over at Lainey, then back at Coop. His nod was resigned, and he turned to leave.

"Rookie." Cooper held out his hand.

Brett frowned, but dug into the pocket of his jeans. "I bet you that you couldn't pick up the girl of my choosing with a lame pickup line. You didn't say I couldn't know her," he muttered, slapping the stack of fifties into Cooper's hand before heading for the doors.

He focused his attention back on the badass who surveyed him with stormy blue eyes.

"So you're Sillinger's sister?"

"Half sister," she countered, hard and fast. "We're not close."

Cooper smiled at the distinction. "Well, you'd be surprised how well he knows you, despite that fact."

She tipped her chin in the direction of the wad of cash in his hand. The fact that her stance relaxed and she uncrossed her arms was not lost on him.

"You bet him you could pick me up with a bad line?"

"He bet me I couldn't pick you up with a bad line."

"Either way, you lost."

Coop stood. He thought for a second she was going to take a step back, but she held her ground. He was impressed. "There's still time to make us both winners."

That startled a cynical laugh from her. "Anyone ever tell you how goddamn cocky you are?"

His grin was wolfish. "A few people."

Lainey rolled her eyes, but all the disdain in the world couldn't hide the slight flush that crept up her neck at her own word choice.

He reached out and grabbed her wrist, turning her palm up. Her eyes widened as he stroked his thumb against the vertical surgical scar there. Her pulse fluttered beneath his thumb, and before she recovered enough to pull away, he placed the two-hundred and fifty bucks in her hand and let her go.

"What's this for?"

Cooper shrugged as he grabbed his jacket from the back of his chair. "Consider it my way of making amends for being stupid enough to believe your brother when he told me he was twenty-one."

Then he thumbed toward the table by the window. "Besides, it might come in handy when they post all those photos they were snapping to social media, in case the liquor board sees you had an underage hockey player in your bar. Take care, gorgeous."

Cooper made a point of not looking back as he walked out.

"WHAT THE FUCK were you thinking?"

Cooper winced at the volume of his agent's outrage. He glanced over at the clock beside his king-size bed. One in the morning. Further proof that Golden didn't give a shit about anyone but himself.

"Did you forget how much Lone Wolf Brewery pays you to drink the bottled piss they are trying to pass off to the world as beer? Because let me assure you, the answer is 'a lot,' Mead."

"I know."

"Oh, you know? Then why the hell is the internet full of pictures of you, in a bar, holding a goddamn highball glass full of not–Lone Wolf beer?"

Cooper pinched the bridge of his nose, reminding himself that Jared Golden had contributed a lot of zeroes to his bank account and that hanging up was not in his best interest. "I didn't drink it."

"Oh, well, great. Then everything's fine. I'll just explain that to the guys at Lone Wolf. Don't worry! Mead didn't actually jeopardize his multimillion-dollar contract with you guys by flagrantly disregarding the exclusivity clause in his contract—he didn't swallow!"

Cooper ran a weary hand across his face. Jared Golden in full panic mode was a lot to take. "I get photographed in clubs all the time. Holding their beer. I'm living up to the deal."

"Jesus Christ, Coop! You *used* to get photographed in clubs all the time. Since you went to Portland, you've been MIA."

"I've been a hockey player. We're getting ready for a championship run here. I have responsibilities to the team."

"You have responsibilities to your corporate sponsors, too! Lone Wolf isn't the only company we're on thin ice with. I spent all day convincing PWR Athletics that you're still the best brand ambassador their money can buy! But I need you on board, Mead. I need you to be seen out and about, and wearing their goddamn T-shirts! You're already behind on media appearances for them, and don't think they haven't noticed. You're on their radar now, and they're going to nail you for every breach of protocol they can find so they can put you out to pasture."

"I'm thirty-two!" The words burst out before he could stop them. Cooper was well aware he was getting up there in the world of sports, but it still rankled. And he was good at hockey—great even. He made sure of it. Which was why he'd devoted more time to training and less time to the gossip blogs lately.

"Exactly. You know the average retirement age for

hockey players? Twenty-eight. We need to make money while you're still a viable commodity! Before they dismiss you and start turning to the new generation. But you need to do your part."

"If you want viable, then I gotta get some sleep. I've got practice tomorrow."

"I'm serious, dude. You need to keep your eye on the prize."

"I'll try not to let *us* down," Cooper said drily.

"Don't be an asshole. You hired me to make you money. And so far, I've fulfilled my part of the bargain. But if you want me to convince another gravy train to pull into the station, you're going to have to do your part. You've only got a few good years left."

Like he didn't know it.

Thirty minutes later, Cooper sat in his GranTurismo S in a deserted parking lot, questioning his sanity.

After he'd hung up with Golden, he'd lain there on his king-size mattress, staring up at the twelve-foot ceilings of his new condo and feeling sorry for himself before he couldn't take it anymore. He had to get out. But when he'd rolled out of bed and pulled on some jeans and a black T-shirt, he'd had no intention of winding up back here.

Of course, when he'd pulled on his black leather jacket and double-checked his hair in the mirror before grabbing his keys, there'd been no doubt The Drunken Sportsman would be his destination.

Now that he was actually there—and judging by the lack of cars, he was the only one—he was rethinking the entire trip. There were a lot of reasons to go back home, but only one to stay. A very compelling reason with long black hair, an intriguingly sharp tongue and an ass that wouldn't quit.

Mind made up, Cooper levered himself out of the matte black Maserati and headed for the door. His security system beeped as he armed it before stowing his keys in his pocket.

Bells on the door jingled as he pushed into the old bar. It smelled like spilled beer and desperation, which he found oddly comforting tonight. Misery loved company, he supposed.

"You've got to be kidding."

Lainey was standing in almost the same spot she'd been when they'd talked earlier, but this time she was hunched over the counter and there was a big textbook open almost to the midpoint on the counter in front of her and a yellow highlighter in her right hand.

"You talk to all your customers that way?" he asked, gesturing to the deserted tables. "In other news, I think I figured out why your bar is empty." Cooper shrugged out of his coat without breaking stride.

She cocked an eyebrow as he approached, recapping the highlighter and stowing it in her apron. Obviously expecting a showdown, she braced her palms on the counter in front of her, on either side of the book. The stance, along with his height, gave him a tantalizing view of her cleavage.

"Oh, you're a customer, are you?"

He slung his jacket on the barstool to his left and held up his hands in surrender. "I'm just here for the beer," Cooper assured her, taking a seat. "Lone Wolf, if you've got it," he said, out of habit. Then, just to shove it to Golden for being a prick, "Actually, give me something imported."

She said nothing as she reached down and grabbed a bottle from an unseen bar fridge. The snap and hiss as she twisted off the cap was the only sound in the cavernous room. For a second, Coop wasn't sure she was going to give him the beer, but after a moment of contemplation, she set it in front of him.

"How much?" he asked, shifting on the stool so he could grab his wallet out of his back pocket.

To his surprise, she shook her head as she tossed the cap into a white bucket beside the sink. "Don't worry about it."

"You sure?"

She nodded, leaning against the counter behind her and crossing her arms over her white tank. "Yeah. Some raging megalomaniac came in earlier and I charged him fifty bucks for unsportsmanlike conduct, so you're covered."

Cooper accepted the jibe, raising the bottle in a mocking toast. "To that guy," he said, before taking a swig of cold, amber liquid.

She bit back a smile, and he was buoyed by the small show of encouragement. "It's Cooper, by the way. Not mega-whatever you said."

She tried to stop it, he could tell, but despite her efforts, there was a slight thaw in her demeanor. "Already forgot my name, huh?"

He rubbed a hand over his stubbled jaw. "Ice Queen, isn't it? Kudos to your mom and dad. It suits you."

Her smile was real this time. Really real, and it kind of made him wish they'd met this way—because of insomnia and liquor—instead of Brett's stupid practical joke. It had been a mistake on Cooper's part. He'd been playing hockey too long to not expect some vengeance from the rookie, especially since Brett had been pretty pissed off when Coach Taggert had given his spot in the starting lineup to Cooper.

He took another sip of beer. "So, Lainey," he said, oddly vindicated at the slight widening of her gray-blue eyes. He'd caught her off guard. "Whatcha reading?"

"Advanced Principles of Marketing." She gave a one-shouldered shrug, as if to say, "no big deal."

He nodded, popping old insecurities that bubbled to the surface. "Not bad. I preferred the sequel."

"Pickup artist and smart-ass, huh? You're a man of many talents."

"For what it's worth, I'm sorry about earlier. I've changed teams a few times in my career. I should have seen through this particular hazing ritual. I know Brett's still pissed I got his spot in the starting lineup. I deserved what I got."

"Yeah, you did." She leaned forward, and this time he knew the flash of cleavage was deliberate. Against his better judgment, the sight stirred his blood.

"But," she drawled, toying with shiny lock of her hair, "there is one way you could make it up to me."

Cooper's mouth went dry. He hadn't drunk enough beer to account for the buzz working its way through his system. It was all Lainey. "Name it."

She bit her lip as she smiled, a secret sort of smile, and it would have dropped him to his knees if he hadn't been sitting on the scarred-up stool. She rounded the bar, and he watched greedily as she made her way to the door. Lainey reached into the black apron that swathed her hips, and the jingle of keys accompanied her journey to the door.

She walked with purpose, fluidly, but controlled, giving the impression that she could handle herself. She had an athletic grace that was sexy as hell. Combined with that body of hers—tight, toned, strong…

Cooper took a gulp of beer to drown his hormones.

She locked the door, flipped the sign so that the closed side faced out. They were completely alone now; there was a weight to that that hadn't been there a moment ago.

Lainey tucked the keys in her back pocket as she approached him, and he was mesmerized by the sway of her hips, the bounce of her breasts. She removed the apron, and even that seemed suggestive, especially when she reached over the bar to drop it on the lower counter and her tank top rode up, revealing a swath of smooth skin that Cooper ached to touch, to nibble, to lick.

Fuck. He pushed the beer away. Maybe the alcohol was affecting him more than he'd realized.

Then she grabbed his hand, tugged him off the stool and said, "Come with me," in a way that made him happy to obey, even before she added, "I've got something for you."

Her hand felt small in his, warm and soft, and he was pleasurably contemplating all the places he'd like to let her fingers roam as he followed her.

Then she took a sharp turn down a small hallway on their left. The bathrooms were on the right-hand side, but she pushed through a door on the left that was marked "Staff Only."

Lainey popped her head back out, and her smile was full of promise. "Just give me a minute?" she begged prettily, and disappeared inside. There was some muffled banging and shuffling behind the door.

Cooper used the brief interlude to check out the mass

of framed photos that lined the wall. They were pictures of the same man—and judging by the haircuts and fashion choices, they spanned at least three decades—smiling as he stood beside some of the biggest names in sports. Cooper was amazed as his eyes bounced from photo to photo—Michael Jordan, Jack Nicklaus, Peyton Manning, Wayne Gretzky.

In fact, Coop was so blown away by the star power on the wall that it took him a moment to realize that he recognized the common denominator in the pictures, too.

"Holy shit! Is this Marty Sillinger?"

"*Of course* you recognize him." Lainey's words dripped with exasperation from behind the closed door.

The pieces clicked together in Cooper's brain with such ease that he couldn't believe he hadn't made the connection before. If the last name hadn't given it away, the fact that Brett wore number 42, just like his old man, should have.

"So you're Martin Sillinger's daughter?"

After a moment of muffled banging and shuffling, she answered. "Yep. Lucky me."

"One of the best enforcers in the league until that back injury put him out of commission. Man, your dad used to go head-to-head with the best the league had to offer. What's he been up to lately?"

"Nothing. He's dead."

Shit. Cooper squeezed his eyes shut at the conversational blunder. It explained a lot about Brett, though. And Lainey, for that matter.

"What happened?"

"Cancer."

"I'm sorry for your loss."

The door swung open with more force than necessary, and Lainey reappeared, stealing his full attention. The flirty smile was gone.

"The guy on that wall is pretty much a stranger to me. After he stopped playing hockey, he wasn't the same. Between the pain meds and the alcohol and the mistress, I lost my dad a long time ago. So you can save your condolences for Brett. And take these."

Cooper was too stunned not to accept two industrial-size rolls of toilet paper in one hand and the bucket containing a toilet brush, cleaner and rubber gloves in the other.

"You're on stall duty." She reached back in the room to grab a bucket of her own, also filled with cleaning supplies, and a pack of paper towels to refill the dispenser. "I'll do the sinks."

Cooper wanted to bail.

Hell, he *should* want to bail.

Why wasn't he bailing?

He tried to list reasons that made sense: long black hair, shiny pink lips, enticingly perky breasts. The list sounded shallow, even to him, because while every single lust-inducing feature was true, deep down Cooper knew the real reason he hadn't walked out.

Jesus.

It was bad news when you were so lonely that you'd rather clean a public restroom in the afterglow of an awkward conversation than go home.

With as much swagger as he could muster, he bowed slightly and gave her the "after you" gesture. She raised an eyebrow, which, if he wasn't mistaken, signified both surprise and something he hadn't been expecting.

He was alone with a gorgeous woman and he'd just

managed to earn her respect. Like his day hadn't gone badly enough already.

His last thought as he followed her into the ladies' bathroom was *fuck my life*.

3

DAMNED IF HE hadn't managed to impress her after all.

Lainey tried to keep her attention on the mirror she was cleaning, but the sight of Cooper Mead in a black T-shirt, jeans and yellow rubber gloves gamely cleaning toilets was too intriguing to ignore.

She'd fully expected him to diva-out and leave her to close the bar in peace. That had been the plan. Instead, he'd ruined everything by making her question if he was more than cocky grandstanding and cheesy pickup lines.

She finished with the mirror and reached back into the bucket, her mind racing as she wiped down the sinks, faucets and countertop while surreptitiously sneaking glances at her assistant.

Hell, Brett had a way of getting under people's skin—she knew that well enough. Cooper's dogged persistence to get her number earlier could definitely have been more an attempt to stick it to Brett than outright douchebaggery.

Something warm flared in her chest, and when Lainey identified it as hope, she knew she was in big trouble.

She scrubbed the ugly green counter with more force. Kind of an "out, damned spot!" thing, and just as futile.

Stupid, she admonished herself. She should have sent Cooper Mead packing the second he walked back into her bar. Instead, she'd foolishly let him stay, and she'd told him more about her father than she'd ever told anyone, and her toilet-cleaning goading had backfired because he'd actually done it, and now she was making excuses for him.

The realization shored her resolve, made her angry. Mostly at herself. "So what are you really doing here, Slick?"

He straightened in the stall—a tight fit for his broad shoulders—and shoved his cleaning supplies back in the bucket. "Insomnia's a bitch," he said simply, punctuating the words with a toilet flush.

She could relate. One of the reasons this bar gig suited her so well. Not that she was planning on keeping it. The second someone made an offer on her late father's ridiculous midlife crisis, she was going to take the money and run.

Lainey kept her gaze on Cooper as he pulled off the rubber gloves and hung them over the side of his bucket before joining her at the sink. The soap dispenser whined out a cloud of grape-scented foam onto his big palm, and he set about washing his hands.

The honesty of the answer surprised her. She gave the counter beside her a last swipe and threw the disinfectant wipe in the trash can. Standing beside him as she washed her own hands, she felt a strange buzz in the chemically scented air.

Cooper reached past her to grab a piece of paper towel from the dispenser, and his arm bumped hers as he tossed the damp ball into the trash can. The innocuous contact hit her like an electrical current, raising goose bumps from her shoulder to her wrist.

She frowned. They were standing in the least erotic of all locations—a public bathroom—and the most innocuous of touches had her all revved up. She had to get out of there. Maybe some space would help.

"We're done here." She grabbed her bucket off the counter and retrieved his from the floor, ignoring the way he held the bathroom door open for her. "You can help me change the keg and then you can go."

She made it an order, hoping he might take issue with it and leave now, but his answer was a genial, "Sure."

She pushed into the janitorial room, abandoning the buckets by the door for the sake of speed, not even caring that she'd get an earful from Aggie tomorrow about how there was a place for everything and *blah, blah, blah.*

Cooper followed her into the bar, behind the counter and then into the back room where the kegs were stored. Lainey unhooked the tap the way Darius had shown her.

"It's a pale ale," she told him, so he could pick the right silver barrel from the stack. Grabbing the empty keg, she moved it out of the way, watching as Cooper expertly maneuvered the full keg into the spot she'd cleared. He made it look effortless, just a quick lift and push. And if his back muscles moved with jungle-cat grace beneath his T-shirt and his biceps flexed with the power of a cobra about to strike, Lainey certainly wasn't affected by it. *Much.*

He flipped the plastic cap off the keg and reached for the coupler.

"You don't have to—"

Cooper glanced over his shoulder and his grin struck

her dumb. "I know you probably won't believe this, but I've tapped a keg or two in my time."

Again, his deft mastery of the task made her skin flush. It was like his hotness was inversely proportional to the size of the area he was in—and, Lainey noticed on a visceral level, they were standing in a very small area. *Self-preservation*, she thought, escaping from the back room to behind the bar, where she could breathe properly.

What the hell was happening here?

"Need me to do anything else?" Cooper walked out of the back room as if he owned the place, all confidence and capability as he closed the door behind him, and that was the last straw.

She hated that she noticed his body—the height of him, the breadth. That she wanted to flirt. Touch his arm again. Run her fingers across all the muscles she'd pretended not to notice.

Because that way lay madness.

That way lay hockey.

"What's your game here, Slick?"

"What?"

His genuine surprise at the attack pissed her off.

"You walk in here like you're God's gift to woman-kind and now that you've cleaned a toilet and changed a keg, I'm just supposed to forget what an asshole you were earlier?" She was coming in too hot; she knew it even as she stepped toward him.

Too much had happened today—too much yelling at Brett, too much talking about her father and too much Cooper short-circuiting her common sense.

Thankfully, she managed to rein in her irrational anger before she poked him in the chest like an insane person.

"What's your problem? Jesus, I told you I was sorry about earlier. What else do you want me to say?"

His chest rose and fell with anger. Dark brows slashed over brown eyes that sparked with heat. Proximity turned the frustration simmering inside her to something else—something hotter—a potent mix of resentment and lust.

She grabbed a fistful of black T-shirt and pulled him down until their mouths were practically touching and the throb in her wrist beat like a drum. She'd broken it a long time ago, but for once it was urging her to focus on the present instead of dredging up the past.

"I don't want you to say anything." Lainey caught Cooper's bottom lip between her teeth, raked them along the sensitive flesh. When she pulled away, their heavy breathing had synced.

Breathing as one, staring at each other, his eyes reflecting the wild desperation that pulsed through her in that suspended moment of calm before she unleashed the angry lust that coursed through her veins.

She smashed her mouth to his, a little too hard, so that his tooth jabbed her lip. But she relished that moment of pain, that tie to reality, proof she was still in control of herself, of the imperfect moment.

Then his tongue traced across her bottom lip, soothing the sting of their lustful collision, and Lainey was lost, swept away in a tidal wave of hormones so potent she needed Cooper—*no, not him*, she reminded herself. She needed sex. That's all this was about.

Lainey kissed him, desperate to keep control, and he drew her to his body—his hard, unyielding body. He was a phenomenal kisser, she decided, slanting her mouth against his. His five o'clock shadow had turned into full-fledged stubble at this late hour, and the rasp of it against her face made her hotter. That little bit of pain-edged pleasure kept things from being too perfect, and made this beautiful train wreck exactly what she was looking for.

Then his hands breached the hem of her tank and she stopped dissecting her questionable life choices and focused instead on the exquisite sensation of his warm palms against her torso.

Impatience surged along with lust, and she tugged on his black T-shirt, revealing abs. Pecs. Arms. He let go of her to tug the shirt over his head and dropped it on the counter.

She pulled him close. Bit his neck, then soothed it with her tongue.

Oh, God, he felt good. Big. Strong. Like he could handle what she was dishing out.

She wanted sex. She wanted to punish him for making her feel this way. For making her want things she'd convinced herself she shouldn't want.

He fisted one hand in her hair, pulled her head back so he could work her mouth. The moment of pain was swept away in something else when his free arm pulled her tight to him.

At five-ten, she'd sometimes considered herself too tall. Right now, though, she was glad for every single inch that put their bodies in such perfect alignment. She wrapped her arms around him, clawing at his back as their tongues dueled, both of them vying for control. When they finally came up for air, Lainey pulled away, needing skin-to-skin contact more than she needed resolution to this petty battle.

Lainey stepped back and yanked her tank top over her head, tossing it on the counter beside his T-shirt.

Cooper's eyes flared as his gaze traced her body, pausing long enough on the contents of her lacy black bra that her nipples tightened at the hungry look in his eyes.

Her breasts weren't overly large, but he didn't seem disappointed—he seemed the opposite, really. And even as her body melted at how beautiful that made her feel, she cursed the inward show of weakness.

Get it together, Lainey. It's just sex.

In a move designed to wrest back control, she reached out and placed her hand against his skin, over his heart. His muscles tensed under her palm. His chest was chiseled and his skin was tanned, even now, in the middle of winter, and Lainey couldn't help but notice that he put the statues she'd studied in her Art History class to shame. Cold marble had nothing on flesh and blood.

She felt the hitch in his breath as she moved her hand, trailing her fingertips down his sternum, across each ridge of his abs, like a mini roller coaster that led down to his belt buckle.

"Do you have a condom?" she asked, tugging at the black leather.

God, she hoped he had protection. She didn't want to retrieve her purse from the locker. She needed this. It had been so long since she'd had sex, since she'd felt that sweet thrill of arousal, since she'd let herself feel anything.

Lainey didn't realize she was holding her breath as Cooper reached behind him. A moment later, he pulled a foil square from his wallet and set both items on the counter beside her right hip. She turned to face them, eyes focused on the condom.

Fucking hockey players, she thought, but there was

no heat to the words, and only the slightest bit of resignation. *Always so damn sure of themselves*.

She lifted her head, and when her eyes met Cooper's in the mirrored backsplash, a shiver of anticipation zipped down the length of her spine. To her surprise, he stepped behind her, and the heat radiating between her back and his stomach was enough to make her knees wobbly. Then he reached around her hip. Thanks to their reflection, she knew he was going to touch her a split second before he did, but the warm, heavy weight of his palm on her stomach still wrung a surprised gasp from her.

In the scratched-up mirror above a bottle of Crown, Cooper's gaze was locked on her parted lips, and her tongue darted out to moisten them. His groan rumbled against her back as the pressure of his hand pulled her tight against him.

The dual sensation of watching Cooper's hand trek down toward the waistband of her jeans and the feeling of his calloused palm sliding down the sensitive skin of her stomach was too much.

Lainey swore as she let her head fall back against his shoulder and closed her eyes.

Everything slipped away—the buzz of the fluorescent lights, the stale smell of beer, the niggling thought that she was in way too deep—everything but Cooper. There was nothing but his solid presence behind her, his fingers breaching her jeans and the warm twist of sexual anticipation thrumming through her body. She reached for her belt, unbuckling it to give him better access and expelled a stuttered breath of pleasure as he accepted the invitation and his hand sank lower, fingers flirting with the lacy hem of her underwear.

She reached for the button, but a familiar twinge shot through her right wrist as she grasped the denim.

Not now, she thought, even as the strength in her thumb waned. *Not right now.*

Lainey squeezed her eyes shut, focusing past the pins and needles. She just needed to undo her pants. She didn't want to think about hockey right now. Didn't want the memories to swamp her. She needed to feel whole, to feel okay, just for this moment.

Cooper's breath against her ear soothed the panic that was blooming through the lust.

"I got it."

And then his right hand covered hers, and the button popped open before he tugged down the zipper. She was ready for him before his hand slid under her thong and then, finally, came the slow, sweet friction she craved. She might have gasped, she wasn't sure, because she couldn't think through the pleasure that swamped her.

All she knew was that his touch was as hot as he was. She could feel his arousal against the small of her back, his breath on her cheek, and his fingers...oh, God, his fingers.

"Yes." The word came out in a weird half moan, half whisper that would have mortified her if her brain were functioning on more than the most basic level. Cooper slipped one broad finger inside her and his groan of pleasure, along with that exploratory thrust, made her knees give out. His arm tightened on her waist, kept her steady even as his words stole her balance.

"I can't wait to be inside you."

He proved he meant it, pressing two fingers into her now, and she was so worked up that the increased pressure had her close, so damn close. She rocked her hips in a slow, sensual rhythm that increased the pressure on her G-spot. Cooper picked up the hint, changing the angle and mimicking her pace.

She reached back, needing to cling to something—raking her nails against his denim-clad thighs as she fisted her hands, desperate to anchor herself in a world spinning out of control.

Cooper ducked his head and pressed his lips against her neck. "I got you. Just let me drive for a while." He twisted his wrist and just when she thought she might die of lust, he pressed the heel of his hand against her clit.

"Oh God, oh fuck!" Lainey couldn't stop the curse words. Unlike most guys, who changed things up when the going got good, Cooper doubled down, and when the sweet shock of orgasm radiated through her, Lainey leaned back against him and, taking his advice, she let go while he drove.

JESUS.

Cooper was desperate for her. Turned on and rock-hard and so fucking desperate.

He'd told her he couldn't wait to be inside her, and he'd thought he meant it—he *had* meant it—but now that he'd watched her come apart in his arms? The words he'd used weren't basic enough; they were too polite for what he needed. He was ravenous for her. He wanted to fuck her until she screamed.

He dragged his mouth up her neck, seduced by the slide of her hair on his chest, the feel of her taut skin under his palms, so soft and smooth. He tugged her jeans down her thighs, doing his best not to be too rough, but she was so damn responsive, and he couldn't breathe through the all-consuming lust she ignited when she leaned forward, placing her hands on the counter in preparation for what was to come.

Then he got his first glimpse of the smooth globes of her ass, bisected by a sexy swath of black lace thong, and he was done for. His cock surged in response, and he freed himself from his boxer briefs and rolled on the condom, shoving the wrapper into his jeans pocket.

He didn't wait. He couldn't.

He slid inside her, and the sweet, hot friction of their bodies wrung a groan from him. Cooper tried to go slow, he did, but even as he told himself to hold on, his hips pumped faster. The slap of their bodies, her whispered curse words and the roar of his blood were the soundtrack to an encounter that was spinning wildly out of control. He dug his fingers into her hips as she used the counter for leverage and pushed back against him, meeting him thrust for thrust.

He ran his hand up her spine, past the clasp of her bra and up the column of her neck. He'd come here expecting a beer, a hard time and temporary respite from his solitude. And now, behind the counter of a run-down sports bar, he'd found heaven.

Cooper caught sight of her in the mirror, and couldn't look away. She was so fucking gorgeous, so wet, so wild for him. He wanted to make it good for her. At least as good as it was for him. Even as his hips bucked, driving deep, he forced himself to breathe deeply, an attempt to keep from blacking out with pleasure as he tried to focus, to learn her expressions as she told him without words how to please her.

When she bit her lip again and reached between her legs, it took everything Cooper had not to come. Not yet. He grasped her hips even tighter, thrusting high and deep, determined to get her there, gritting his teeth against the exquisite sensation when her fingers brushed his cock as she drove herself to the peak and then she opened her eyes and looked right at him, and finally, finally, he felt her fall over the edge, her muscles pulsing against his cock, legs trembling as he pumped again, and then one more time, his climax hitting hard and fast, wringing everything from him.

He'd never…it had never been like this before. And it wasn't just the fact that she might be the first woman he'd been with who didn't porn-moan. The mirror had allowed him watch her expression change, shifting from anticipation to determination to pleasure. He knew, could tell, she'd never meant him to see all that. That she'd forgotten her reflection was selling her out, the way people forgot you could see them singing in their car, that the glass couldn't hide their love of disco.

And he wanted more.

She straightened, hair sexy and tousled, and Cooper reached for her, because he couldn't help himself, but she sidestepped his embrace, adjusting her thong and tugging her jeans up her thighs with a series of cute little hops. She struggled for a moment with the button of her jeans, and he let her. She'd made it plenty clear she only needed him for one thing, but as her movements grew less sure, more panicky, he couldn't just stand by.

"Can I—"

"It's fine," she bit out, buckling her belt over her still-unbuttoned jeans. Lainey pulled the zipper up awkwardly with her left hand before she turned to grab her tank off the counter.

Cooper frowned at the dismissal, discreetly taking care of the condom. "Okay, sure. Then maybe we could grab something to eat?" He tugged his jeans into place. If sleep had been elusive before the adrenaline surge he'd just experienced, well… Besides, dinner had been hours ago. "Is there an all-night diner around here? I'll buy you some eggs."

He didn't think he'd ever invited a woman to breakfast after a one-night-stand, but he didn't stop to analyze his motives.

"I have to close up the bar." Lainey pulled her tank top over her head and tugged down the hem.

"I can help," Coop offered, fastening his jeans and pulling his belt back into place.

"You've done enough. It's not a two-person job," she told him, and though he wasn't wild about the idea of her in this place alone in the middle of the night with a bunch of cash, he reminded himself that she'd probably locked up a thousand nights before.

"Look, Slick. Tonight was great. The sex was great. But that's all it was—a night of great sex. So stop trying to turn it into something more."

She busied herself by grabbing a rag from the sink and wiping the counter down, but Cooper got the impression it was more about avoiding eye contact with him than any actual need for cleanliness.

"Lainey, c'mon. I didn't propose marriage." He pulled his T-shirt on, then ran a hand back and forth across his hair. "It's just breakfast."

She looked at him then, but there was no coyness in her eyes. Nothing flirty. "I don't date hockey players."

"Yeah. Okay. Right." Cooper shrugged, trying to let her rejection roll off his back. No big deal. He'd eat alone. He preferred it that way. It wasn't like he was looking for a relationship or anything. He'd just thought…hell, he didn't know what he'd thought. "Just sex. That's the best kind, right? Well, it was a pleasure meeting you, Lainey Sillinger."

"Harper. I took my mother's maiden name."

"Harper. Got it," he relented with tip of his head, grabbing her phone off the counter as he walked by. He was relieved to see it didn't require a passcode.

"Hey, give that back!"

"Just in case you change your mind and get hungry later," Coop explained, texting himself a quick message as he stepped out from behind the bar. "And word to the wise? You should lock this. Anyone could pick it up and check out whatever naughty videos you've got stored on here."

He came to a stop beside the stool where he'd left his jacket before relinquishing her phone. She practically lunged at the counter in her haste to snatch it. With a grin designed to rankle, he picked up his coat and he headed for the door.

"Cooper?"

He stopped. There it was. Something vaguely like relief flooded through him as he turned to face her.

"That door is locked. You mind going out the staff entrance in the back?"

"No problem." He shook his head, hoping it didn't look as robotic as it felt, even as he followed in the direction she was pointing, past the storage room she'd been coming out of when he'd first laid eyes on her. It felt like a lifetime ago, though it had only been hours. A short hallway with doors on either side brought him to a beat-up metal exit door, and he pushed through it to find himself standing in the parking lot, next to a Dumpster, about ten feet away from his car.

It had been a hell of a day.

4

THE EAR-SPLITTING SHRIEK of the whistle echoed through the chilly arena air, and the rest of the ambient noise—the scraping of skates, the tapping of sticks and the boom of pucks hitting the boards—faded out.

"Okay, guys, last drill of the day. Let's make it count." Coach Taggert's heavy baritone echoed down the rink.

Cooper stood by the boards, elbow resting on the end of his hockey stick, watching as center Eric Jacobs—or Cubs, as he was better known to his teammates—turned on the jets and blew past the rookie on the outside. But instead of hustling back into position, Brett slammed his stick on the ice, upset at getting beat.

That pulled Sillinger's defensive partner out of position, and Cubs capitalized on the defensive error by sending a beauty of a cross-crease pass to a wide-open Luke Maguire, who easily tapped the puck into the net.

It was all Cooper could do not to roll his eyes as the kid swore and flung his glove at the boards, not even having the grace to look embarrassed when he lumbered over to stand beside Cooper.

"What are you looking at?" Brett demanded, all littleman swagger as he unsnapped the chin strap on his helmet.

"Jesus Christ, Rookie. Get it together. And pick up your glove. You're embarrassing yourself." Cooper's softly worded chastisement deepened Brett's frown.

"Don't call me Rookie! Everyone still calls me 'Rookie' even though this is my second year."

"Then stop acting like one." Cooper banged his stick on the ice a few times to dislodge the snow on the tape of his blade. "Jacobs beat you fair and square. Man up."

Brett reached down and scooped up his glove. "Easy for you to say. You took my spot on the first line. Every time I screw up, it's good for you. It means you don't have competition."

Okay, now the kid was pissing him off.

"I don't know if anyone explained this to you, but we're on the same team, so when you screw up, that's bad for all of us. And just for the record, you could be playing your best and you still wouldn't be competition for me. Because I'm better than you."

Brett's *fuck-you* look was oddly satisfying to Cooper.

"Look, you're a good hockey player. You wouldn't be here if you weren't. But you're here to play hockey, not to be a hotshot. You're not thinking about the team. You're just thinking about yourself. Nobody gives a shit if Jacobs blows by you sometimes. It happens. It's happened to all of us at one time or another. That's the game. But if Jacobs blows by you, and you break formation, and we cover for you but you don't have our backs because you're out of position, then we're screwed."

"Everything okay here, Mead?" Luke Maguire skated up, skates hissing against the ice as he stopped.

Cooper nodded at his captain. "I'm great. How 'bout you, Rookie? You good?"

Brett shoved his hand in his glove, gave a terse nod and skated back to line up for the next drill.

Cooper and Luke shared a knowing look. "Were we such punks when we started out?"

Luke shook his head. "I wasn't. You definitely were, though."

The joke earned Mags a punch in the shoulder as he skated away. Then, after a moment of hemming and haw-ing over whether he should get involved, Cooper gestured Eric Jacobs over.

He blamed the lapse in judgment on the fact that he felt kind of sorry for Sillinger and what he'd gone through. Pro hockey was a different world. Hell, some-times Cooper *still* found it tough to navigate. He couldn't imagine how it was for Brett, who seemed to be going it alone. And after losing his father at nineteen...

Cooper and his father might not see eye-to-eye on everything, but he knew if he ever needed Walter Mead, he'd be there. Brett didn't have that luxury.

"Do me a favor. Next time you're on the line against the rookie, run it the same way with the wide left swing. I want to see if he learned his lesson."

Eric nodded, pushing his helmet up his forehead with the thumb of his glove. "Sure thing. I'll beat him again, though."

"You know that and I know that. I need the kid to know it, too."

Eric nodded thoughtfully. "Once he figures it out, he's gonna be pretty good."

"That's the goal. Let's just hope it sinks in before you get old and slow."

"Well, we only have six years before I catch up to you, gramps, so we'd better get a move on." Eric slapped Cooper in the shin pad with the blade of his stick before he skated back to the center line to rejoin the offensive drill.

Twenty minutes and one intensely frustrated Brett Sillinger later, the whistle blew again.

"Okay, good practice today," the coach said. "I want to see all of you at the team lunch because someone from PR wants to go over some things before we head to the autograph session at the mall. Now go hit the showers. Not you, Mead. I want to talk to you."

Damn, damn, damn.

"Sure thing, Coach."

The team filed off the ice, and Cooper pulled off his helmet and gloves, balancing them on the edge of the boards so he could shove his sweaty hair back off his forehead.

"You know why I called you over?"

Cooper had a sneaking suspicion, but he decided playing dumb was the better option. He raised his eyebrows and gave a shrug of his shoulder pads.

Judging by Taggert's knowing look, he wasn't buying it. "There's a photo of you in a bar that I'm told is making its way around the internet."

"Oh. That."

"Yes, *that*. And normally, I wouldn't even mention it. But little things, well, they have a way of leading to bigger things, and we can't have that, Mead. Not this year. I…" The gruff bulldog of a man paused to clear his throat. "I trust you know what happened here last season?"

He was referring, of course, to one of the biggest scandals in hockey—hell, in sports in general—to make the front page in recent years. The team's goaltender, J. C. Lacroix, had been nailed for throwing games to clear up his gambling debts and had received a lifetime ban from hockey and a helluva fine, and there was still the potential for jail time.

The Storm organization had spent the entire summer being poked and prodded and investigated to make sure the bad-apple syndrome hadn't spread before they got the okay to play this season. The fact that they'd not only been cleared but were on the brink of making a playoff run was nothing short of a miracle.

Coop nodded.

"Then you also know we're under the microscope this year. We need to not only play better than the competition, we need to be above reproach on and off the ice." Setting his clipboard on the bench—it was old-school hockey all the way for Taggert—the man sighed, giving Coop a rare glimpse behind the hard-ass reputation.

"We need you on this team. We need your experience. That's why we made the trades we did. But because of our situation, we also need a guy who's bringing the right kind of attention to the team. A guy with his head in the game."

"Understood." Cooper grabbed up his helmet and gloves and swung a leg over the boards, joining his coach in the players' box. "And believe me when I say, I want a championship as much as every man on this team." The sincerity in his voice seemed to ease some of the worry on his coach's face. "You can count on me."

"I'm betting on it." Taggert rubbed a hand over his craggy jaw. "And Mead?"

Cooper stopped, seconds away from making a clean getaway to join his team in the dressing room.

"You've been around long enough to know you never take a rookie to a bar."

Busted.

"Yeah, about that. He's legal in Canada, and sometimes when I get homesick, I forget your exotic American customs. Won't happen again, Coach."

Taggert's white brows dipped low into a frown. "It damn well better not, after the tongue-lashing I gave him on the subject this morning. Which, uh, brings me to the other reason I wanted to talk to you. I know the kid can be a bit much to take. He's had trouble making friends on the team because he's a lot younger than most of you. But he looks up to you, Mead."

Coach shoved his hands into the pockets of his navy Portland Storm jacket. "And, well, what you did for him out on the ice during that drill? I was hoping you might consider doing a bit of that with him off the ice, too."

Surprise widened Cooper's gaze. "Give him a hard time?"

"Mentor him. The kid's got potential but he needs a nudge in the right direction."

Sillinger needed a body check in the right direction in Cooper's opinion. *Geez.* He was barely keeping his own life together. He wasn't interested in nannying the rookie.

But that wasn't the sort of thing you told your coach after a direct order masquerading as a heart-to-heart, so he just nodded and headed for the showers, hoping his "I'll see what I can do" was vague enough to absolve him of the need to actually do anything.

THE DAY LAINEY had been waiting for since she'd arrived in Portland had finally arrived, and all she could think about was sex.

She was supposed to be celebrating, dammit! She'd even had Darius pour her a beer.

The real estate agent she'd hired to sell The Drunken Sportsman had brought by a serious client that morning, and judging by the sheer number of words the woman had repeated—"The client is very, very interested. He really, really likes the location. I feel so, so good about this showing"—the bar was as good as sold. Lainey didn't even need to shell out for the cosmetic upgrades she'd planned for the space.

But as Lainey sat there, nursing the mug of pale ale, she wasn't reveling in her looming triumph. She was remembering the play of Cooper's muscles beneath his T-shirt as he switched out the keg for her. The intensity in his eyes as he drove into her body, never breaking the connection they'd made in the mirror as he'd pushed her toward mindless pleasure and joined her in the free fall.

Lainey pressed a hand to her abdomen to settle the flip of her stomach. He was overbearing and cocky as hell. But he was also charming. And funny. And obsessed with breakfast. And *so damn hot*.

She tried to silence her hormones with a mouthful of beer, avoiding the aforementioned mirror that mocked her from her seat at the bar.

She was glorifying it. She had to be. She'd had plenty of orgasms before. Good ones. The white-hot pleasure she'd experienced with Coop was just a false memory.

Probably.

But there's only one way to be sure, a little voice inside her head whispered.

After all, Lainey rationalized, reaching into her purse to pull out her phone, she was celebrating. And selling the bar meant that she'd be back to her hotel consulting gig within a week, maybe two. After that, they'd never see each other again. Hell, with playoffs about to start, they probably wouldn't see each other after tomorrow. All things considered, it was the perfect time to just get him out of her system and be done with him.

He'd said she could change her mind when he'd hijacked her phone yesterday. As she tapped through to the screen she was looking for, her fingers tingled with the phantom memory of the first time they'd touched, that jolt that had been such a weak preview of what was to come.

Lainey opened the conversation to find that he'd texted himself a single character: the spider emoji. She knew she was in trouble when she realized that she was sort of pleased that he'd chosen something relevant. She would have expected a bunch of cheesy hearts...or the eggplant.

No. No emotions allowed, she reminded herself. *Just sext him and get on with it.*

About to leave the bar and could use a ride. Interested?

She reread the double entendre.

Too dirty, or not dirty enough? Maybe he'd just think her car had broken down. She added the eggplant emoji for clarity. Deleted it. Did the same with the winky face. Mentally chastised herself for putting so much effort into this, and hit Send before she could overanalyze the whole thing more than she already had. Lainey set her phone on the counter and took a gulp of her lukewarm beer, marveling at her own bravery. She'd just bootytexted Cooper Mead.

She checked her phone. No reply.

She played a half-hearted round of the word game she'd downloaded. Spent some time spinning her beer mug in a slow circle. It was still half-full but too warm to drink. She pushed it away, rested her cheek in her hand and watched her bartender mix drinks for a while. Much as Darius sometimes got on her last nerve, he was actually a pretty decent—she pounced on her phone when it buzzed on the counter, punching in her passcode with record speed…to find that her supervisor at Zenith was reminding her—*again*—that she needed to log in to the work portal and choose her next assignment if she didn't want one assigned to her.

Deleting the text, she frowned. So he was playing hard to get, was he? Punishing her for sending him away without breakfast?

Well, she'd just see about that.

Just thinking about all the things I want to do to you tonight.

Lainey nodded smugly. He wanted to play games? She could give as good as she got. Cooper Mead might think he was making up the rules of this little flirtation they had going on, but she would show him she was not to be underestimated. She was going to leave, and if he showed up at the bar before her next text arrived, with directions to her hotel room, all the better.

Shoving her phone in the back pocket of her jeans, she stood, and placed a few bills on the counter to pay for the beer. She checked her phone once—phantom vibration— before grabbing her purse and heading for the back door.

The thought that he might be waiting in the parking lot for her, wearing jeans and a white T-shirt, leaning against the hood of whatever fancy car he drove like a stereotypical bad boy from an old movie stopped Lainey before she reached the exit. She ran her fingers through her hair, wet her lips and readjusted her bra. With a deep breath, she pushed through the door.

Cooper wasn't there.

It was only nine o'clock, she reminded herself as she walked to her car. Still early. Maybe he hadn't checked his phone yet. She'd hear from him soon.

By ten o'clock, she'd sent a total of six naughty messages, triple-checked that her phone wasn't on mute, shaved her legs while perched on the edge of the hotel tub, changed into sexy red panties and a white tank, and come to the realization that Cooper wasn't going to drop by and take the edge off.

She flopped back against the pillows on the hotel bed. She was angry, yes, a little bit embarrassed, maybe, but more than that she was restless. She'd worked herself up sending that string of racy texts. Remembering Cooper's big, calloused hands on her skin, imagining all the things she wanted to do to him when she had him in front of her, horizontal and naked, with nothing but time on their hands.

She shifted her bare legs against each other, enjoying the soft slide of skin against skin, the slight increase of pressure between her thighs. She was keyed up, turned on, sexually frustrated to the extreme. She looked over at her silent phone.

Fuck it, she decided. Grabbing it, she typed, I'm starting without you, and shimmied herself under the covers. He'd had his chance, and if he wasn't interested, so be it. In fact...

She tapped through to her video recorder and looked

into the camera, her eyebrow cocked with challenge as she hit record. "Should've answered your texts, Slick," she said, before angling the camera toward the sheets that covered her lower body. Slowly, she ran her hand down the white cotton tank, across her stomach and under the sheets.

The comforter moved as she navigated the waistband of her underwear, and she took great pleasure keeping them hidden from the camera. She'd put them on for him, but if he wasn't going to fulfill his end of the bargain and show up, then he didn't deserve them.

She couldn't help the satisfied exhale as her fingers settled right where she needed them. She bit her lip as she indulged in the slow, sweet friction that she craved. Her body was primed for pleasure, responding immediately to the glide of her fingers.

She could take care of herself. She didn't need Cooper Mead to do it for her.

The thought reminded her of the phone in her left hand, and she angled the screen back toward her face. She was flushed, hair spread out across the white pillow case, her breath coming faster as she touched herself. She'd planned to say something scathing and turn off the camera, but there was something wicked about recording herself in this most intimate moment, something hot and sweet that wound its way through her veins and amped up her pleasure. Her lips curved into an indulgent smile, and Lainey reached over and propped the phone against the alarm clock. With a final glance at the screen, Lainey rolled onto her back and gave herself her full attention.

She was already wet, thanks to her earlier fantasizing about Cooper, though it rankled a little that he was in any way responsible for the crescendo building below decks. Still, it would be a shame to waste such a nice sexual buzz. Lainey rolled her hips, sucking in a breath as sparks tingled deep in her gut.

"Oh, God."

It felt good. Better, hotter than usual. And yet, it was a pale imitation of what she'd wanted this evening. Her eyes drifted shut, and she moaned softly. A slideshow of Cooper's hands on her body, fingers gripping her hips as he drove into her, played through her mind, and the memories made her insides tense.

Pulling her knees up, she slid one finger deep inside herself, and the change in sensation ratcheted up the tension in her belly. She remembered—hell, how could she forget?—the heat of him, the leashed power of his big, muscular body behind her. The intensity in his eyes as he watched her respond to his every touch in the mirror.

She slipped another finger inside. It didn't ease the ache, such a poor replacement for his fullness, the power of having him inside her, filling her and pushing her closer to the brink with every stroke. She was close, so damn close. The orgasm was right there, within reach, and she clenched her thighs, straightened her legs, twisted her hips. Lainey ran her free hand across her stomach, up to her breast, squeezing as she increased the speed of her fingers below the sheets. Then she pressed the heel of her hand against her clit, like he had, trying to recapture the magic of his touch...

Oh, Jesus. "Coop..."

White light flashed behind her eyelids and her back arched and she drove her hips high as a rush of pleasure shook through her body, leaving her limp and sated in its wake.

Lainey took a few moments to catch her breath before she rolled onto her side and reached for her phone. "Sorry you missed out," she told him, before she stopped the recording. With the press of her thumb, she attached the video to a text and hit Send, watching the spinning circle as the data transferred.

When her phone indicated that her message had been delivered, Lainey couldn't help smiling. She felt powerful. As though she'd freed herself from a toxic addiction to Cooper Mead. A big middle finger to the man who twisted her up inside. The emancipation felt incredible.

For about thirty seconds. Which was approximately when her brain reminded her that that empowering, self-induced orgasm she was so proud of? It had come courtesy of the graphic memory of his hands on her body.

Dammit.

Lainey lay there for a long moment, staring up at the ceiling.

Luckily, he didn't have to know that.

5

COOPER FOUGHT BACK a wave of nausea and disorientation as he woke up in a pitch-black room. He reached blindly toward the end table for his phone, and the movement made his stomach roil, so he rolled himself onto his back and lay still for a long moment as his body readjusted and calmed down.

How long had he been out?

He'd spent four hours at a meet and greet with Portland Storm fans in some mall he couldn't remember the name of. It had meant sitting elbow to elbow with teammates, inhaling Sharpie fumes and scrawling his name on hats, jerseys, T-shirts and a surprising number of breasts. And while the turnout had been amazing, Cooper much preferred meeting fans more organically, like at the bar, because these days, most people preferred chatting and taking a selfie with him, and he didn't have to worry if they spelled their names with a "K" or a "C" or a "CH" or a silent "W."

These more formal events involved a lot of writing, and a lot of spelling, and that sort of concentration always did a number on him, physically and mentally. It made him feel like he was back in school, back to being the stupid kid, hunched down in the back row, hoping he wouldn't get called on. The day he'd graduated—by the narrowest of margins—and left books and homework behind had been the best day ever.

Autograph sessions were the one time his dyslexia still had the power to ruin his life.

His last lucid memory was of arriving back at his penthouse suite with a monster headache around six in the evening. He'd headed straight for the bathroom to swallow some pain pills, and then shed clothes until he fell into bed in his underwear intending to sleep his way through the thrashing in his skull. He'd managed to turn off the ringer on his phone and hit the remote-control button that engaged the blackout blinds on his massive, south-facing windows. He must have passed out minutes later.

His head was still tender, like he had a headache hangover—better, but with just enough phantom sensation to remind Cooper of how much it had hurt. Not that he was surprised. With a deep, steadying breath to calm the acidic feeling in his stomach, he made another grab for his phone and this time he was successful. When the screen lit up he recoiled from the brightness, allowing his eyes a few seconds to adjust before he opened them again.

The digital readout said it was quarter after eleven. In the morning.

Damn. He'd lost over twelve hours to the worst headache he'd had in recent memory. He'd also slept through about a hundred text messages. The mere thought of reading them made his brain throb. There were also seven missed calls, all from teammates, four of them from Luke. Why the hell was everyone…

Oh, shit.

Coop rolled out of bed and bolted for the shower. He was supposed to be at the children's hospital in fifteen minutes. There was no way he was going to make it on time. Coach had already warned him about the need to keep up appearances. This was the last community event before the playoffs started, and there would be a lot of press there, compiling feel-good stories for the six o'clock news.

After walking through the spray, Coop toweled off and brushed his teeth simultaneously, and was still pulling on his T-shirt as he headed out the door.

By the time he arrived at the ward, out of breath, hair still damp from his shower, he was relieved that he was only half an hour late. He was less relieved that every one of his teammates was decked out in a Portland Storm jersey. *Whoops.* Cooper flagged down a harried-looking blonde woman carrying a clipboard and wearing a lanyard with team credentials on it. "Hey, some kid just spilled juice on my jersey. Any chance there's an extra I can borrow?"

"Of course! I'll find you one immediately," she told him, barely pausing as she made a note on the clipboard before hurrying off to put out the next fire.

With that taken care of, he glanced around the room, taking stock.

A couple of the guys were doing interviews with perky, smiling television reporters, but most of them were scattered around the large common room, buddied up with kids and their parents, playing ping-pong and video games if they were able, reading books and shooting the breeze if they weren't.

Cooper snuck around the perimeter of the room, away from the activity, to the quiet space where the kids who'd been wheeled into the room still in the hospital beds were hanging out. He caught his captain's eye just as Luke was finishing taking a photo with a little girl with a bright, gap-toothed smile and a smooth, bald head.

He watched as the girl's grateful mother gave Luke a hug. These visits were always a stab in the heart, no matter how many Cooper attended.

"Where have you been? I tried calling a bunch of times." Thankfully, Luke sounded more concerned that angry.

"I slept through my alarm. My phone was on mute. I'm sorry I'm late, man."

"You're gonna be sorrier when someone from PR sees you're not wearing your jersey."

"Already taken care of."

"Sign this for me."

Cooper caught the hat Luke tossed to him. "This might be taking your hero worship of me too far, Maguire. And before you beg, forget it. I'm not putting any hearts before my name."

"Just make it out to Melissa and stop being a smart-ass."

Cooper uncapped the Sharpie. The scent alone was enough to make his brain give a terrified throb at the prospect of more autographs. After this, he was going to find a dark corner to hang out in for a bit, and then he'd implement a selfies-only rule.

With intense concentration, he made an "M" with a scribble after it before he scrawled his own name, adding a fairly legible 16 at the end. Luckily, being a hockey player didn't require good penmanship.

"Melissa, eh? Let's grab dinner after this and we can talk about how much money it's going to cost you to keep me from telling your super-hot girlfriend about this mystery woman," Cooper joked.

"Hate to rain on your retirement plan, but my super-hot girlfriend already knows about her, because Melissa is her nine-year-old niece. And we're having dinner with her at Holly's dad's place tonight, which is why I need the hat," he explained, grabbing it back and whacking Cooper in the shoulder with it. "She is going to flip out when she gets this. You're, like, her fifth favorite player. After me and some other guys who are way better than you."

"Luke, sorry to interrupt, but we're ready for your interview." The blonde woman Cooper had spoken to earlier about the jersey appeared out of nowhere and whisked Maguire away.

Cooper recapped the marker and holstered it in his back pocket.

"That's Luke Maguire. Number 18. Left winger. Team captain. He has sixty-three assists this year."

Coop turned in the direction of the small voice behind him, his eyebrows raised with genuine surprise. "He does?"

The kid nodded, but there was a solemnness to him as he pushed the glasses back up his freckled nose. He looked tiny, resting in a hospital bed that had been angled so he was mostly sitting up.

"Huh. That's pretty good."

"Second highest in the league."

"I'm glad he's on my team." Cooper glanced around the room. "You know if there's anywhere to get some food around here? Like a vending machine or something? I'm starving."

The kid reached over the rail of his bed and pulled up a backpack featuring a cartoon moose playing hockey.

"Sweet backpack."

The boy sent a derisive look in Coop's direction as he unzipped it. "It's for babies. I picked it out in second grade, but I'm ten now." He rifled around for a minute, before producing a Ziploc bag full of crackers shaped like fish. "Want some of these?"

"You talked me into it." Cooper grabbed the empty seat next to the bed and accepted the snack bag gratefully, tugging open the seal while his benefactor rezipped his pack and dropped it back over the edge of the bed.

"These are delicious." Cooper tossed a handful of the orange carbohydrates into his mouth, and held the bag out so the kid could grab some, too.

They sat in silence for a while, munching on crackers and taking in the sights. Ten minutes passed before the kid spoke again, but once he started, there was no stopping him.

"That's Eric Jacobs. Number 2. Centerman. He's tied for fourth-highest scorer, even though he missed twelve games at the beginning of the season because of a knee injury." He moved his finger a couple of degrees to the right. "That's Brett Sillinger. Number 42. Defenseman. His plus/minus is the lowest on your team at -14." His finger tracked right again. "That's Tyson Mackinaw. Number 31. Goaltender. His save percentage is 0.921."

Cooper tried not to laugh at the derisive tone despite the better-than-average stat. "You don't sound impressed."

"He was better at this time last year."

"Tough crowd. What's your name?"

"Danny."

"So how do you know all this stuff, Danny?"

"I like hockey. Sometimes my treatments make me feel sick, so it hurts my eyes to watch TV, but I can listen to the radio. And my mom reads me stuff from the magazines. And the internet." He lifted his shoulders and hands in a shrug of wonderment. "I just remember it."

The ubiquitous blonde lady appeared again, this time carrying a jersey. Cooper held up a hand to signify his new position, and she changed course abruptly, coming at them like a heat-seeking missile. Coop leaned toward the hospital bed. "Hey, if this lady asks, tell her you spilled juice on my jersey, okay?"

"I'm sorry it took so long. There were a couple of media issues, and then I couldn't find you." She held the jersey out to Cooper, but before he could thank her, Danny chimed in.

"I spilled juice on his jersey."

The lady nodded, but she was already scanning her checklist for the next box to check off. "That's nice. Have fun, you two."

Cooper slung the jersey over the armrest of his uncomfortable chair and turned to face Danny. "Thanks, partner."

"Now you have to do me a favor."

Cooper laughed. This kid was a real shark. "It's only fair."

"Will you read me some of this?" He leaned forward and pulled the playoff edition of *Hockey News* from behind his pillow.

A familiar anxiety tightened Cooper's chest, and he

forced himself to take a few deep breaths before he took the magazine, flipped through a couple of glossy pages.

"You, uh, you sure you wouldn't rather play ping-pong or air hockey or something?"

Danny shook his head, and the droop of his shoulders was heartbreaking. "I get tired fast."

Cooper felt for the kid. It was exactly how he felt about trying to read right now. He did his best to let them both off the hook.

"So do I have to find my own stats in here, or do you know who I am?"

"Cooper Mead. Number 16. Defenseman. You shoot left. Traded from New York to Portland in a blockbuster deal for Viktor Alfredsson and three draft picks. You're thirty-two, you grew up in Red Deer, Alberta, Canada. You were drafted first round, thirtieth overall. Right now you're tied for the top-scoring defenseman in the league with twenty-one goals."

"Wow. You weren't kidding. That's a helluva memory you've got there."

Danny's eyes widened and he had to push his glasses up again. "You said *hell*."

"I did."

The confirmation earned him a frown.

"You're not supposed to swear."

"Says who?"

The kid looked at Cooper like he was stupid. *"Everyone."*

"Well, I'll tell you a secret. Sometimes everyone is wrong. I mean, I was supposed to wear a jersey to this thing, but if I had it would mean that I wasn't late and then I wouldn't have been lying low in the back corner, and then we never would have met."

"And I'd still have some crackers left."

Cooper knew when he was beat. "Touché, kid. But instead of reading a bunch of stats and arguing about who ate whose crackers, how about you and I talk? Ask me anything. Take advantage of the fact you're sitting here with the best defenseman in the league—"

"Third best defenseman in the league."

Cooper frowned at the assessment. "Man, you really do like stats, don't you?"

"I like how they can predict stuff. Stats are like seeing into the future."

Cooper tossed the magazine back on Danny's bed.

"Stats are bullsh—crap," he said. "You know how I know?"

"How?"

"Because they say I'm the third best defenseman in the league."

Danny looked skeptical. "If you think you should be number one, then you need to improve your plus/minus."

"What I mean by that," Cooper continued, undaunted by the sarcasm, "is that at any given moment in any given game, I might be the third best defenseman in the league. But sometimes I'm the best. Sometimes, I might be the tenth best. Because ultimately, it doesn't matter what the stats are. What matters is what you do in the moment, you know?"

Danny's mouth twisted into a contemplative pucker as he thought about that for a moment. "You're also a meme."

"Excuse me?"

"You know when a photo goes viral and people write funny stuff on the picture?" Danny asked, pulling a cell phone out of nowhere, his tiny thumbs flying over the device with a speed Cooper found enviable.

"I know what a meme is. What do you mean that I'm a meme?"

"You're all over the internet. You're even trending on Twitter. Hashtag barfail. It's pretty bad." The kid's dire tone rankled as he turned the screen around as evidence.

"You think?" Cooper grabbed the phone, scrolling through endless shots of him holding that goddamn Black Widow, his face folded into a disgusted sneer, all captioned in the obnoxious white block letters that ruined people's lives.

THAT FACE WHEN YOU'RE CHEERS-ING 15 YRS IN THE LEAGUE WITH NO CHAMPIONSHIP.

WHEN YOUR FUTURE'S SO BLEAK YOU DON'T GOTTA WEAR SHADES.

Oh, man. This wasn't good. Especially on the heels of Taggert's "right kind of attention" chat. Probably explained at least half of the texts he was still ignoring. Golden, on the other hand, was likely drinking champagne. The T-shirt Cooper had worn to the bar was PWR Athletics and the logo was visible.

Jared just didn't understand that this trade to Portland was about so much more than preserving endorsement deals. It wasn't about the money.

This was about being a kid watching *Hockey Night in Canada* with his parents and realizing that if he put everything he had into it, he could be on that screen one day.

Cooper had always dreamed of having a championship ring on his hand. The sad fact was, he was running out of time. His body wasn't going to last forever. His slap shot was bound to fade. And after he was done playing hockey…well, he tried not to think about that too much. But he had a real chance this year, of living out his boyhood dream of playing in the big game, of hoisting hockey's greatest trophy over his head, sweaty and battle-weary and triumphant.

That was all he'd ever wanted, since he was ten years old. Danny's age.

This was the year he would make that dream a reality, and he wasn't going to let anything distract him from that. Not bad publicity. Not rejection from a gorgeous bartender. *Nothing.*

But first…

"Danny, you ever watched a *Rock'em Sock'em Hockey* video before?"

He shook his head and Cooper handed back his phone.

"Pull that up on YouTube. I'm gonna blow your mind."

Two hours and a whole lot of body checks and mid-ice collisions later, Cooper and Danny said their goodbyes, and Coop was back in the colorless hospital lobby, heading for the exit with Eric beside him. "Don't suppose you want to grab some food?"

"I would, man, but Rebecca and I—"

"I get it."

"Next time though. Oh, shit." Eric's entire body seemed to freeze before he reached the sliding doors that led outside.

Cooper stopped next to him, but he couldn't tell what had caused Cubs's standstill. There was a small congregation of Storm fans, wearing various logo-emblazoned apparel, from hats to shirts to jerseys. A couple of the guys from the team were still caught in the crowd, posing for pictures and autographing things. It was pretty much business as usual.

"What?"

Jacobs gave a dismissive shake of his blond head. "Nothing. Let's go," he said, resuming his pace toward the door. Cooper walked on, but when they went through the first set of the sliding doors, Eric crossed behind him so that he was on Cooper's left side.

"Mead, when we step outside, just know that I respect you, both as a hockey player and as a man, and I'm sorry for what I'm about to do, but I'm already late to meet Rebecca, and I don't have time to deal with this right now."

His words coincided with their first step out of the hospital doors, and before Cooper knew what had happened, Jacobs had given him a firm shove to the right, and he bumped hard into someone who squealed. Cooper reached out automatically in an attempt to steady his victim.

"Oh, my gawd! I can't believe Cooper Mead just, like, literally knocked me off my feet."

"Uh. Yeah. Sorry about that." After he knew the woman had regained her balance on her extra-high heels, Cooper let go of her waist, though she clung to him for a transparently long time before finally letting him go with an unnecessary squeeze of his biceps. "You okay?"

He caught Jacobs's eye—the prick was steadily making his way through the fan gauntlet and offered nothing but a mouthed "I owe you one," and a weak shrug before he turned to smile for the next picture.

"Janelle."

The voice pulled Cooper back to the situation at hand.

That, and the fact that the *situation* was tracing the ridges of his biceps with her purple talons. "What?"

"My name is Janelle."

"Right. You okay, Janelle?"

"I'll live. I don't mind when things get a little rough."

Oh, man. Eric's speech made complete sense now. Not that Coop didn't recognize a clingy puck bunny when he saw one. He was a sacrifice, and now Eric was free to make his getaway and Coop was tangled in the kind of web that could be difficult to get out of. Jacobs was going to pay for this. Cooper would spare him no mercy next time they ran a checking drill at practice, that was for damn sure.

"Ok. Well. Nice meeting you." There'd been a time when he would have taken Janelle up on what she was offering. A time that wasn't that long ago. A perk of the job, he used to say. But it wasn't enough anymore.

She stepped closer. "What, you ran into me, but you don't even have time for an autograph?" she asked, tipping her head to the side and giving him flirty sad eyes.

"Sure. What did you want me to sign?"

He watched with perverse fascination as she uncapped the Sharpie that had materialized from who knew where—her little black dress was too tight to hide much—and held it out to him. He took it and she leaned forward, tugging the neckline of her dress down a bit farther, although there was already more than enough skin exposed to fit his entire hockey résumé.

When he'd temporarily branded his name on her exposed cleavage, he capped the pen and handed it back, but it was another ten minutes of politely declining her various invitations to "hang out" before he managed to slip away. He posed for a few more pictures with some genuine hockey fans before he finally made it to his car.

Cooper ran a weary hand down his face.

He tried to remember when this had gotten old, having beautiful women throw themselves at him. In theory, it was still awesome. And yet...

Coop pulled his keys from his pocket and unlocked the door before he folded his large frame into the leather interior of the Maserati.

The truth was, he envied Eric. Luke. All the guys who had somewhere to be because someone special was waiting for them.

Leaning forward, he pulled his phone out of his back pocket. The message light flashed incessantly, but he ignored it, tossing the phone onto the passenger seat.

His first order of business was to find some dinner. Then he'd check his messages.

6

COOPER WAS TUCKED into a table in the back corner of the little Vietnamese place a couple of blocks from his condo. His doorman had recommended it and Cooper had been ordering takeout on a weekly basis since he'd moved in. The place was a little hole in the wall, with sparse decor and a built-in-the-sixties vibe, but their pho was hard proof that not all the good food was in New York.

He popped in his wireless headphones, and had already erased his dozen or so voice mails by the time the elderly owner shuffled out and set his giant bowl of soup on the Formica tabletop. In addition to his teammates' calls wondering why he was late, there were a couple of messages from Jared Golden, one praising the meme— all publicity was good publicity in Golden's eyes—the other bemoaning the fact that, in all the coverage of the children's hospital visit, Cooper hadn't been featured in a single interview.

Cooper dug into the soup with a set of plastic chopsticks. He was so hungry that he wolfed down half the noodles and a good portion of the exquisite broth before he finally came up for air. Those fish-shaped crackers had been hours ago.

He grabbed his phone, intending to let his stomach adjust to the novelty of digesting food while he scrolled through the text messages. There were too many to read even if he *hadn't* had dyslexia, so he vetted them by sender, deleting with abandon. But when he noticed that the contact photo of the spider emoji had double digits next to it—what was that? Twelve? Twenty-one?—curiosity got the better of him, and he thumbed through to the message screen. A bunch of blue text bubbles appeared, but Cooper's eyes were immediately drawn to the video message, and he hit Play.

An angry Lainey filled the screen, her black hair fanned out around her on a white pillow, her eyes stormy as she raised an eyebrow. "Should've answered your texts, Slick."

And then the most incredible thing happened.

Cooper swallowed hard as the camera panned past her breasts, obviously braless beneath her white tank top, and he forgot to breathe as her hand snaked under the covers. He felt her contented sigh all the way to his core as the blankets began to move ever so slightly.

"No fucking way."

The woman at the next table frowned at him, but he barely noticed.

He wasn't this lucky. The Ice Queen had not sent him a sex video. It was a joke. She was going to turn off the camera the second he was hot and bothered. But seconds kept passing, and she was still on the screen. Thanks to the superior sound quality of his ear buds, every sexy moan and shuddered breath made his body tighten, made the blood in his veins roar with lust. Then she raised the camera from the sheet back to her face, and she stared at him, eyes drowsy with desire, and it turned him inside out. It made him want to touch her. To get the fuck out of this restaurant and go back to his place so he could touch himself.

But he didn't. Because even though the sight of her made his body scream for release, he knew this video was a punishment, and he respected the hell out of that. The sounds she made, the way she bit her lip, her eyes drifting shut to savor the pleasure she was giving herself. Pleasure he should have been giving her, if he hadn't been chock-full of painkillers and battling a monster headache.

Everything about the video was perfect. It was even hotter that he couldn't see what she was doing. In this era of 24/7, on-demand porn—name your fetish, we've got it all—there was something so titillating about seeing the results of the actions taking place under the comforter, but being left to imagine them for himself.

Hell, he couldn't *stop* imagining them.

And then she bit her lip and moaned his name as she came apart, and his cock flexed painfully against his jeans, and he banged his fist against the table as he wrestled to stay in control of his body. He needed to get the hell out of here before he died of lust.

After a couple of deep breaths to calm his raging hormones, he tossed a twenty on the table and made a beeline for his car.

He folded himself into the bucket seat, pausing to drop his forehead against the steering wheel. When he thought of how he could have spent last night…

He couldn't believe he'd missed her booty texts for the most clichéd reason. "Not tonight, dear. I have a headache." Jesus. He knew it was the truth and it *still* sounded lame. But he had big plans to make it up to her, to make it up to himself. Because if that was what happened when she was alone, well, just wait until he got his hands on her.

Coop turned the key, gunning the engine as he pulled away from the curb.

COOPER WAS DAMN lucky he hadn't gotten a speeding ticket on the way over. He'd punched it on all the straightaways and played fast and loose with a couple of yellow lights, but it was all worth it as he swung the sleek black sports car into a parking spot. He forced himself to keep a regular pace as he strode across the lot, but when the moment of truth came, Cooper paused at the glass door, staring at the peeling letters that at one time had heralded the name of the bar but at this point only proclaimed the "runken Sp rtsma."

His exhalation was longer than it should have been. The last time he'd seen Lainey, she'd been coolly dismissing him from her life. He ran a hand through his hair and tugged at the hem of his T-shirt.

Ridiculous. Just walk the fuck in.

And yet…something had changed. Hell, *everything* had changed. That goddamn video—he got hard just thinking about it, about her—had fucked him up. The prospect of seeing her was…no big deal.

He ran his palms down his jeans.

Man up and walk in!

Cooper pushed on the door and stepped inside. Lainey's head snapped up, as if she knew it was him, and her gaze was like a kick to the gut. The bartender said something to her, and she turned away from him to load drinks onto her tray.

For the first time, he noticed that the place was moderately busy. Instead of standing in the entrance like a moron, he slid into a seat at the nearest empty table. The Trail Blazers game was blaring on every screen, monopolizing everyone's attention and obviously keeping Lainey busy. Which was a relief, because he needed a moment to compose himself before she took his order.

His original plan, which he now realized had been some variation of shoving her up against the nearest wall and fucking her until she moaned his name the way she had in the video, wasn't an option in their current surroundings. Maybe he could sneak behind the bar and pull her into the storage room full of kegs, and then—

"Oh, my gawd! Cooper? What a coincidence!"

Oh, no. Not the time, and definitely not the place for this.

"Hi!" The woman's toothy smile faltered slightly at his complete inability to form words.

He understood why Eric had made him a sacrificial lamb now. This girl was no joke.

"Janelle." She pointed at her boob, where the black blob of his signature marked her skin. "Remember?"

From an hour ago? Uh, yeah. He did. Which was why his stomach had filled with dread. "Yeah, good to see you again. Listen, I need to—"

"I was totally hoping to see you again, too. Such a weird coincidence that we'd both end up here, right?" The way she said it led Cooper to believe it wasn't a coincidence at all. Pictures of him in the bar were all over social media, both from his impromptu autograph session for the sports fans by the window, as well as his infamous meme. The jaded part of him wondered if she'd driven straight here from the hospital, hoping he'd show.

"Mind if I join you?"

"Actually, now's not the best—"

She ran her hand across his shoulders and down his arm as she sat in the chair beside him rather than the one across from him. "I'm, like, so glad you're here. I hate to drink alone, you know?" She turned in her seat, snapping her fingers in Lainey's direction. "Oh, my gawd. This waitress is, like, seriously the worst. Hello?" Janelle waved her hand around. "Hell-ooo!"

Lainey had just dropped off a round two tables away, and her gaze cut toward them like a razor.

"Okay. She's finally coming over. Honestly, it's like she was ignoring us on purpose or something."

"Yeah," Coop agreed, astounded by the complete obliviousness of his parasitic companion. "I wonder why that would be."

Sarcasm was obviously lost on Janelle, as her response was a wide-eyed shrug.

"You beckoned?"

God, she was beautiful. His body stirred at the sight of her, and he had to squeeze his hand into a fist to keep from reaching for her. The fact she hadn't made eye contact was not lost on him.

"It's about time you got here. We've been waiting forever, haven't we?" Janelle looked to him for confirmation.

Cooper shook his head, disavowing the statement, but there was acid in Lainey's voice when she spoke. "What can I get you?"

Janelle wiggled in her seat, smacking her gum. "What's the special tonight?"

"Beer."

"Ew. Beer is like, so gross. What are you having?"

It was on the tip of Cooper's tongue to say beer, but he didn't want to encourage Janelle or piss off Golden, and Lone Wolf was the last thing he felt like drinking tonight. "Just water for me."

Janelle's pout was impressive. He figured she was probably the type who'd used her Instagram feed to perfect it.

"Playoffs start the day after tomorrow."

Her eyes lit up, and she shot Lainey a smug smile. "Cooper plays hockey. Professionally."

"You don't say."

The total lack of interest obviously disappointed Janelle, but she regrouped. "I want a fun drink. Do you have any fun drinks?"

Lainey looked pointedly around the bar, as if drawing attention to the beer-and-wings vibe. "You mean something with an umbrella in it?"

"Yes! What do you have that's like that?"

"Nothing. We don't serve drinks with umbrellas."

"You're, like, the worst waitress I've ever—"

"She'll have a Black Widow."

Lainey and Janelle both stared at him, but Cooper was so relieved to finally have Lainey's attention, he didn't even care that she was frowning at him.

"Ooh. That sounds delicious!"

"It's a secret menu item. Fifty bucks a glass." Coop pulled out his wallet, and when he handed over the bill, he brushed his fingers against Lainey's. It felt good to touch her, even chastely, and when he cocked an eyebrow, gesturing subtly at his companion, he could have sworn he saw her stifle a smile.

Not one to be ignored, Janelle heaved a sigh that seemed designed to test the strength of the material keeping her breasts in check. "Isn't it so super hot when your guy orders for you?"

"It's the dreamiest," Lainey agreed, tucking the money into her pocket. Cooper was sure that her demeanor had thawed now that she knew he didn't welcome Janelle's intrusion any more than she did.

"What's her problem?"

A giant cheer in response to something that had happened in the basketball game saved Cooper from having to answer. He kept his eyes on the screen for a few minutes, relieved not to have to make small talk. But Janelle wasn't going down without a fight.

"Oh! I didn't get a chance to take a picture with you earlier. Do you mind?"

Since her phone was already locked and loaded in selfie position, he didn't think his opinion mattered.

"Uh. Yeah. Okay." He leaned in until he could see himself in the screen of her rhinestone-studded phone. As expected, her duck-face-game was strong.

"One more!" she insisted, before he could straighten up. "I think I blinked."

She hadn't, but Cooper knew how to read a play. Sometimes it was best to go with the flow. He pasted his media smile back on, but this time she turned her head at the last minute and kissed him, mostly on the cheek, but she'd caught the edge of his mouth.

She licked her lips, her eyes half-closed. "Just a little something to remember me by."

"Here's your drink." Lainey slammed the water glass in front of him. And just like that, the rapport they'd established was gone. She put Janelle's drink on the table with slightly less force and took off toward the back door of the bar.

"What a bitch. Hey, where are you going?"

Cooper didn't answer as he pushed away from the table and followed in Lainey's wake, but when he burst through the door and into the parking lot he couldn't see her anywhere.

A metallic creak jerked his head to the right, and he found her, standing beside the Dumpster near the back entrance, one hand supporting the heavy lid so she could toss a garbage bag into its reeking depths. When she let go, the lid crashed down with a bang.

"I think I lost her," he joked, thumbing behind him.

Lainey didn't react, just turned her head to stare at the sky. Streaks of pink and yellow were starting to appear against the deepening blue. Cooper took a moment to soak in her profile, from the top of her head down the slope of her nose, but when he reached her lips, which she'd painted a glossy, deep red tonight, looking wasn't enough anymore. He took a step toward her.

"I got your message." His voice was deep, almost hoarse, with restrained passion. Being alone with her for the first time since he'd watched the video had sparked a need in his belly that was proving difficult to ignore.

She lifted her chin, and the stubborn set of her jaw struck a discordant note in his lust-muddled brain.

"That offer expired. You should probably get back inside before you miss your date's inevitable nip slip."

Cooper frowned. "You know I'm not with her, right?"

Lainey sent him a withering look. "Why would I care if you were? We barely know each other."

She pulled a set of keys from the pocket of her apron and stepped past him, unlocking the door they'd just come through.

"Come on. Lainey…"

She paused for a second in the doorway, but when she raised her eyes, there was hurt in them.

"Wipe the lipstick off your face."

Cooper lifted his hand to the side of his mouth as the door slammed shut behind her.

7

SHE'D MADE GOOD TIPS.

That was the one bright spot in an otherwise vomit-inducing night. Lainey sighed, flicking on her left turn signal as she pulled to a stop at the last light on her way home. She could see the prestigious logo of Hotel Burke in the middle distance, and she couldn't wait to crawl into bed and put the evening behind her. Little Miss Black Widow had hung around for a whole hour before she took the hint that Cooper wasn't coming back, and Cooper, well...

The light changed to green and Lainey accelerated through the left turn, clearing the deserted intersection. When she took the final right turn into the parking lot, her only thought was, *oh, shit*.

Because standing there, leaning against his sleek black sports car like a bad boy from an old movie, was Cooper Mead. And just like she'd predicted, he looked damn good doing it.

His T-shirt was black rather than white, and she used the small deviation from her fantasy to steel herself against the fact that he'd ditched what's-her-face to stand in a hotel lot and wait for her. She never should have texted him the address, let alone that video.

She parked her car next to his, and made sure to slam the door when she got out, so he knew she was pissed. "You've got to be kidding me."

"Did you honestly think I could stay away after that video?"

Lainey hiked her purse up her shoulder, crossed her arms and looked away in self-preservation. She wasn't going to fall for his pretty words, no matter how earnestly he delivered them. "Do me a favor and save the shitty romantic comedy lines for your bar floozy."

He shot her a pointed look, and she rewarded his attempt at humor with a scowl. "In case you're in the habit of accosting so many women in bars that you can't keep us all straight, I wasn't talking about me."

Cooper pushed away from his car, raising his hands in surrender. "No more jokes. But I think we need to talk about this."

"Maybe I haven't made it clear enough, but I'm not interested." She strode to the door of her hotel and into the lobby, well aware he was only a step behind. The well-trained desk clerk made a move to save her from her stalker, but Lainey waved him off. She could deal with Cooper Mead on her own. Still, she made a mental note to raise the percentage on the "Anticipates Guests' Needs" portion of her report before she sent it in.

Cooper waited until she'd stopped at the elevator and turned to face him before speaking.

"You were interested last night."

The look on his face was so damn sexy that she spared a moment to mourn what could have been if he'd just shown up when he'd been damn well supposed to.

She pressed the button a few times in quick succession. "Like I said, limited time offer. You missed out. I took care of things."

"You sure as hell did."

The growl in his voice made her knees weak as she stepped into the elevator.

"I didn't make that video for you. I made it for me."

He nodded, joining her. "I know."

A flicker of surprise lifted her brows as the elevator doors closed, and she cursed herself even as she schooled her face into a haughty but neutral expression and pressed the button for the third floor.

"I've watched that video a hundred times, Lainey. Watched you touch yourself with one hand and give me a figurative middle finger with the other. That's what made it so goddamn sexy—you were so focused on yourself, on your own pleasure. Letting me know with every stroke what an asshole I was for not texting you back. Showing me what I was missing without giving a fuck about me watching you... I get hard just thinking about how hot it was to see you like that. You were so beautiful."

Her scoff was full of bravado, and she had the disconcerting feeling that he knew it. That she'd somehow given herself away by the quick dart of her eyes and the heat in her cheeks. She took a step back, but only one, before raising her chin. "Please. You think you can come in here and smooth-talk your way back into my life? You missed your chance, Slick. The clock ran out before you took your shot. That's how it goes sometimes." It bothered her that she didn't mean a single word of it.

"You know what turned me on the most? The sounds you made. Every whimper, every sigh, every moan—I can still hear them. I want to hear them again."

She was this close to letting him, to shoving him up against the wall and allowing him to make good on all his pretty words. The door slid open, but since her room was directly across from the elevator, it wasn't much of a reprieve.

"I'm kicking myself for missing those texts, Lainey. But let me give you what you asked for last night."

She reached into her purse, liberating the key card. "It's not going to be easy to make it up to me."

"I'm up for the challenge."

"That's a lame, overplayed joke." She swiped the card and stepped inside, but to her surprise, he didn't follow her in. He just left her holding the door as he propped one broad shoulder against the jamb.

"It's not a joke. It's the truth. In every way. Invite me in."

She hesitated at the switch in tactics. His full-court press had worked. The second they'd stepped into the elevator together, she'd known she was going to take what she'd wanted so desperately last night. What she still wanted. But this? What the hell was he doing? By her calculations, she should already have her legs wrapped around his waist, the path to the bed strewn with clothes. Lainey hated that he could throw her off balance so easily.

"What, you're a vampire now? Can't come in without permission?"

Her taunting didn't faze him. What made him a great defenseman was that he'd learned to read the game and not fall for the deke. *Damn him.*

"Invite me in, Lainey."

Something in the tone of his voice made the hair on the back of her neck stand up. It wasn't fear that trickled down her spine, though. It was a sense of danger, pure and simple. The kind that kicked up a girl's heartbeat and made her knees spongy. It was the good kind.

Lainey swallowed. Cooper took up the whole doorway, all broad shoulders and brooding sensuality.

"Why should I?" Her breath might be shaky, but her words weren't, and she was thankful for that.

"Because I want to touch you. I want to figure out every dirty thing you did to yourself under that sheet. I'm going to learn what I need to do to get you to make each and every one of those noises. Every moan, every gasp, every stuttered breath. I want to figure out your body. I'm going to make you say my name again."

It was suddenly very hard to breathe. "I didn't say your name."

The rapacious glint in his eye made her doubt her statement.

"I want to make you scream with pleasure, and I want you to invite me in so you know that you want that, too."

Oh, God. "I want that, too." *Did she ever.*

She'd expected him to pounce, slam her up against the wall, but he just stepped over the threshold, closed the door behind him. There was a finality as the dead bolt slammed into place, and the scrape as he slid the chain home sent nervous energy skidding down her arms. She hugged herself against the sensations churning in her gut.

Then he turned and fixed her with a predatory look, and her arms fell to her sides. What had she done?

His gait was slow and purposeful. Coop had a loose-hipped, athletic swagger that was sexy as hell. He stepped closer—close enough for her to catch his warm, male scent, close enough to feel the heat radiating from his large, muscled frame. So close that if she took a deep breath, their chests would touch.

"Those were some pretty big promises you made back there."

He tipped his head forward, his lips a hair's breadth from hers, but not making contact. She swayed toward him involuntarily, unable to resist their magnetic pull. "I'm a man of my word," he said softly, before finally, *finally*, giving her what he'd made her admit she'd been waiting for.

The fleeting brush of his lips stopped her breath. He did it again, and once more, as though he liked wielding that power.

"Lainey?" He ran his fingers up her arms slowly enough to leave a trail of goose bumps.

"Mmm-hmm?"

"I want you to take off your pants now."

She stiffened at his imperious tone, but he swooped in and kissed her before she could argue.

"I told you what I was doing here and you invited me in. That means that tonight we're playing by my rules. Now take off your pants."

Lainey shivered at the command. There was a part of her that was galled by his autocratic demeanor and smug orders. But there was another part of her, too…the part that was tired of making decisions, tired of being strong all the time. And that part was desperate to play along, to take the pleasure he offered, and to let him take control. It was just for one night, she assured herself, as she reached for the button on her jeans.

Her wrist cooperated, and she kept her gaze on his beautiful, rugged face as she slid the zipper down, slowly, seductively, she hoped. She might be playing by his rules, but that didn't mean he held all the power, as evidenced by the way he clenched his jaw as she shimmied her jeans down her hips.

Cooper tugged the black satin panties down her thighs and pushed her onto the mattress. Lainey found herself lying back against the pillows with her unbuttoned shirt hanging open to reveal her matching black satin bra and a dangerously intent Cooper Mead between her legs.

Her pulse beat an elemental rhythm and he hadn't even touched her yet.

"I've been waiting for this," he confessed. The soft, low timbre of his voice set off a tremor in her belly. Without conscious volition, she drew her knees up, further exposing her to his gaze, and the way his eyes darkened as he moved closer increased the thrum of excitement coursing through her veins.

She was wet for him. Desperate for his touch. His words built a hunger in her so fierce that her world had narrowed to a pinpoint of pleasure.

He stroked his thumb across her most sensitive flesh, and the shock of pleasure was so good, so sweet, that she cried out.

He rocked his fingers inside her, applying the most delicious pressure to her G-spot at an angle she couldn't match on her own. Her breath came faster as the pressure built.

"Jesus, Lainey. You're so fucking sexy."

She rewarded him with a moan as she fisted the sheets on either side of her hips. God, he was good at this.

And then Cooper's other hand brushed her clit and Lainey's hips bucked off the bed at the current of electricity that jolted through her. "Oh, fuck. Coop."

"Come for me, baby."

She wanted to—goddamn, she wanted to—but even in the midst of the deep, curling pleasure, the sexy command made her question giving him everything. She didn't want to need him. Not even for this.

"Seriously, Lainey?" Cooper read the tiny change in her body and slowed the pace of his fingers. "Take what I'm trying to give you. Let me make you feel even half of what watching you in that video made me feel."

The sweetness of his words, even as they got down and dirty, melted her last little fortress of resistance, and her body relaxed.

And that was when Cooper, the king of patience, finally pounced. He twisted his fingers deep inside her, and instead of replacing his thumb on her clit, his play-off stubble abraded the sensitive skin of her inner thighs as she tightened them around his head and the sudden wet heat of his tongue shocked her into orgasm, and she fell over the precipice, saying his name again and again as she came apart.

8

COOPER WOKE UP naked and alone after the best sleep he'd had in a long time. He stretched against the sheets and took stock of his surroundings—king-size bed, upscale furnishings, state-of-the-art TV. Pretty nice digs Lainey had secured for herself.

His assessment made him realize that he'd been playing hockey long enough that he barely noticed the differences between hotel rooms when he was on the road anymore. They'd all blended together into one featureless room that felt more like home to him than his Portland condo did. Probably the reason he'd slept so well last night.

Well, one *of the reasons he'd slept so well*.

The other was nowhere to be seen, but her suitcase was on the small desk by the window, so he figured she hadn't made a run for it. Cooper grabbed a quick shower, and was in the process of getting dressed when he heard the hotel room door swing open.

Lainey tossed a fast-food bag at him when he stepped out of the bathroom, and he caught it against his bare chest.

"I know how much you love breakfast." She set the cardboard drink tray on the closest end table and pulled one of the cups free. "Coffee?"

"Yes, please." Coop walked over to her, accepting the to-go cup, and pressed a kiss to her forehead. "You are a goddess."

She blushed slightly and turned her head, grabbing the other coffee as he settled himself on the bed, back against the headboard. He dug through the bag, but there was only one breakfast sandwich inside. "You're not having anything?"

"I already ate mine," she told him, taking a seat on the bed next to his feet.

Cooper tried not to be bothered that she'd made a point of eating alone as he unwrapped his meal.

"Slick, no. Come on. Why do you look disappointed right now? I brought you food."

"I just thought I could take you out for breakfast. But this is good." He held up the sandwich. "Thanks for thinking of me." Cooper indulged in a mouthful of greasy deliciousness. He probably should have turned it down and had something healthier, but what good was training like a beast if he couldn't indulge every now and again?

"These are some sweet accommodations you've got here."

She glanced around the room as though she, too, was seeing it for the first time. "Job perk. When I'm not restoring my absentee father's dive bar so that it's fit to sell, I travel the country as a hospitality consultant."

Coop paused midbite. "That's a real job?"

Her frown said that it was.

"And what exactly does a hospitality consultant do?"

She shrugged. "All kinds of stuff. Basically, hotels

hire the company I work for to secret-shop them—I stay there, assess the staff, the cleanliness, the food, the amenities. Then I write up reports and action plans so they can work on their weak points and exploit their strong ones. Depending on their budget, sometimes I stay and implement staff training programs."

"So your entire job is to go from place to place and be super critical of people." He nodded to himself. "Actually, it explains a lot about you."

"Like you get to cast aspersions? You chase around a piece of rubber and hit people for a living!" She chucked a pillow at him, and he laughed.

"I meant it in a good way!"

"You did not," she countered, but her wry grin let him know she wasn't offended. "But it's been good. A perk of being one of Zenith's top consultants is that I get first dibs on which jobs I want to take, so when I inherited the bar, I requested all the gigs in the area. That way I'd have a place to stay while I sold the bar, and I would stay in good standing at work."

"Win-win."

"It should have been. But this bar is taking forever to sell. If I can't unload it soon, I'm going to have to look into hiring someone to run it until I get an offer."

She took a sip of her coffee. "This assignment ends in a week, and my supervisor is all over me to pick my next job, or she'll pick one for me. I've run out of Portland hotels to grade, so it's time to hit the road again."

"It must've been nice to be in one place for a while."

"Actually, I kind of miss being on the move. Portland is a bit suffocating, don't you think?"

Cooper used to feel that way, knew that craving to get to the next destination. Now, he wasn't so sure. He was starting to like the idea of feeling more at home at his place than in a hotel.

"Actually, I like it a lot more than I thought I would."

They stared at each other for a long moment. Lainey looked away first.

"You working at the bar today?" he asked, following his question with another bite of breakfast sandwich.

She shook her head. "Nah. Taking the day off." She took a sip of caffeine. "How about you?"

"Nothing on tap. Last day of freedom. Playoffs start tomorrow."

"Fun." Her accompanying smile was so fake that he had to laugh.

"What's your beef with hockey anyway? Your dad obviously loved it."

Lainey's look was a perfect marriage of scorn and disbelief. "And you're citing that as a 'pro' in the hockey column?"

"Your brother plays."

"He's my half brother."

"I just think you'd like it if you gave it a chance." He reached for the coffee he'd set on the end table and took a slurp. His mouth was suddenly dry. "Our first two games this round are at home. You should come to one. I can get you tickets." Cooper was aiming for nonchalant. He just hoped he'd landed somewhere in the general vicinity, because the alternative was desperate.

Lainey looked surprised at the offer. "I heard playoff tickets were sold out."

"When you're on the team, there are ways of getting them."

"Oh." She was looking anywhere but him. "Well, thanks for the offer, but I don't think so."

Cooper told himself it was a muscle twitch, not a flinch. He took another giant bite of his sandwich.

"I told you before, Slick. I don't do hockey."

"You said you didn't do hockey players either," he pointed out, his crass attempt at levity earning him a frown.

"I said I didn't *date* hockey players. And we are not dating." Lainey frowned, more to herself than at him. "You're just so into having breakfast together. And me coming to watch you play. It sounds like a man looking for a girlfriend, and I already told you I'm not into that."

Was he?

He had to admit, the idea was not without some appeal. Maybe he was ready to settle down a *little*. At least spend more than one night with someone.

"So that's why you won't let me take you out to breakfast?" he asked, finishing off the sandwich and shoving the wrapper back in the empty bag.

"That's part of it. I just… I'm not interested in the life you lead. Cameras in your face all the time. Reporters shoving microphones at you. People hounding you for autographs only to go and talk shit about you on the internet afterward." She shrugged like it was no big deal, but there was a bit too much force behind her words.

She wasn't telling him everything. Her dad had played professional hockey when Lainey was a baby and the internet wasn't even a thing, so it couldn't be fallout from that. And Brett and Lainey weren't close enough that she could be angry on his behalf—the rookie was too small a fish in the sports world to have made much of a splash yet.

"It can be a little overwhelming sometimes, I guess, but honestly it's not that bad. I mean, being a pro athlete isn't quite like being an actor or a rock star. I mean, sure, a few people recognize me here and there, stop me for a quick photo. More often than not I just get some double takes, sort of a 'that guy seems familiar,' but they can't quite place me. Most people just walk by. Unless there's a group of sports fans congregating, I can usually pass for a normal person."

She chuckled, and though it was a little forced, he was relieved to see her lighten up. She was so damn serious all the time. "Just throw on some sunglasses and a hat and see how the other half lives, huh?"

He grinned. "Exactly. In fact, let me prove to you how unglamorous my life can be. Let's go somewhere. Hang out in the world."

Lainey gave him a look of exaggerated contemplation as she took another swig of her coffee.

The seconds that ticked by felt like hours.

"Okay. But I get to pick the place," she stipulated.

The knot in Cooper's gut loosened, and he exhaled a breath he hadn't meant to hold. "Lainey, you've got yourself a deal."

COOPER SHOVED HIS hands in his pockets and tried not to look bored. They'd been in the used bookstore for a ridiculously long time. The library smell of the place was giving him horrible flashbacks of research essays and homework.

"Isn't this place the best?"

"I guess so." Cooper reached into one of the bins and pulled out a beat-up pulp fiction novel that had a picture of a Tyrannosaurus rex brandishing some sort of space blaster and shooting up buildings. After inspecting it for a moment, he tossed it back on top of the pile. "Books aren't really my thing."

"Too cool for school," she said with a knowing grin, as she adjusted the four massive textbooks in her arms. "I should have known."

It was a playful jibe, but that was exactly the way he'd made it through his school years. Pouring every moment into hockey, into training, into impressing his classmates until his bad grades meant nothing and his on-ice prowess made him one of the popular kids. Until he was a quintessential Canadian jock, his sights set on the big league, on hockey superstardom. And he'd done it, he reminded himself.

Which was why he was standing there with a smart, beautiful woman teasing him. And she could say what she wanted about not wanting to live her life in public, but he knew that if his life was more private, she wouldn't be standing with him now. Fame was his smokescreen, the disguise he donned to keep people from discovering his weaknesses. She didn't know, he reminded himself. He'd kept his dyslexia under wraps for over a decade. There was no reason his chest should feel tight.

Cooper reached over and grabbed the books from her. "I'll carry them."

Her smile softened and she glanced away from him, the tip of her dark ponytail brushing his biceps. They started meandering toward the cash register. "How about you? Judging by the weight of your purchase, I'm gonna guess you were a straight-up nerd."

She smiled sweetly and gave him the finger before stopping to flip through yet another huge book with a spine that was three inches thick.

"No one buying these books skipped university."

She glanced up from her perusal of the tome and he leaned one elbow on the top of the shelf beside her after a casual shrug.

"College. Whatever you Americans call it."

She laughed at that. "Yes, our Americanisms are so exotic and difficult for you foreigners to grasp. How long have you lived here now?"

Cooper grinned, realizing that hanging out in a bookstore with a sexy, intelligent, smart-mouthed woman might not be quite as boring a way to spend an afternoon as he'd originally thought. And that he was genuinely curious to know more about her.

"Okay, college girl. Spill. What did you study? Did you have a sordid affair with your professor? Did his tweed blazer have elbow patches on it?"

"I went to college. No illicit affairs, despite the prevalence of tweed and elbow patches. After the divorce, Mom and I were on our own and money was tight. I didn't want my mom to have to live paycheck to paycheck anymore. A degree in commerce seemed like the way to go. And it fostered my obsession with textbooks." She lifted the one in her hands as evidence.

The answer surprised the hell out of him. Even with a midrange contract, Martin Sillinger should have been able to take care of his daughter and ex-wife.

"What happened with your family?" he asked.

Lainey sighed as she closed the book and shoved it back on the shelf, but he saw the way her shoulders slumped. "It's a long, sordid story, rife with clichés."

"I've got time."

For a moment, he thought she was going to tell him, but then she lifted her chin and shuttered the pain in her eyes. "Things change. The end." The finality in her voice was reinforced by the quickening of her pace as she resumed their earlier trajectory toward the cashier.

Cooper was so taken aback by the abruptness of her departure that he had to jog a few steps to catch up with her, despite his longer legs. "Lainey?" He hoisted the books into a more comfortable position against his forearm. "Talk to me."

She stopped, turned to face him, looking so fragile that it made his chest ache. "I—"

"Elaine? Elaine Sillinger? Is that you? Oh, my gosh! Hi!"

Cooper and Lainey both turned toward the intruder, a stocky blonde woman with short hair and a toothy smile. Coop could feel the tension rolling off Lainey as she stiffened beside him, and the sudden pallor of her skin made it clear that she did not share the woman's joy over this unexpected reunion.

"Shelly Harris." Lainey's voice sounded brittle.

"Shelly Gardner now!" The blonde held up her left hand, pointing unnecessarily at the massive rock adorning her finger. "Kent and I weren't even going to get married, and now we're total suburbanites—two kids, a dog, a minivan, the whole deal."

"Congratulations."

Shelly smiled bigger, which Cooper had doubted was possible a moment ago. "Thank you. I'm really happy. And you? What have you been up to? I haven't seen you since...wow, since Vancouver, I guess. Are you still playing hockey?"

Cooper's gaze snapped to Lainey as the bombshell dropped. She blinked a few times, opened her mouth, but nothing came out. Cooper took a step forward. "She doesn't. I do. I keep trying to convince her to come watch a game sometime, but I'm not having much luck." He held out a hand, and Shelly's eyes widened as she shook it and he didn't get a chance to introduce himself.

"Oh, wow! Cooper Mead. I'm so sorry. I didn't mean to be rude. I was just surprised to see Elaine. It's great to have you playing for Portland. We needed some defense. My husband is going to die when he finds out I met you. Do you mind?"

She held up her phone, and Cooper dutifully ducked into the frame beside her.

"Elaine, get in here! I want a photo with you, too."

A few snaps later, Shelly had stowed her phone but was still talking a mile a minute.

Cooper didn't like the dazed, not-quite-there look on Lainey's face.

"I can't wait to let the girls know I ran into you! Lindsay still holds a team reunion every year, but we've never been able to find you." Shelly glanced conspiratorially at Cooper. "Your girl is a ghost on social media. Impossible to find. But seriously, Elaine. You should totally come this year."

Lainey's wan smile was all Coop could take.

"Well, Shelly, it's been a pleasure and I'm sure Lainey would love to stay and catch up, but we're late for a dinner thing, so…" Cooper elbowed Lainey, and the shove broke her stupor.

"Yes. Dinner thing. I'm sorry, Shelly. We've got to get going. But it was nice to see you."

"Okay. Well, stay in touch. Really good to see you."

Lainey grabbed Coop by the arm and tugged him forward.

"I'm on Facebook!" Shelly yelled after them.

"You play hockey?" Astonishment lifted Coop's

brows. "How did I not know this about you? I mean, way to bury the lede!"

"I *played* hockey. Past tense."

"So the Ice Queen title…you're telling me that isn't just about idiotic bar patrons."

Lainey's expression was one of sad resignation. "It is now. But no, it didn't used to be."

She looked up at him, her gray-blue eyes damp and mournful, and the bleak expression made him frown.

"What's wrong?" He put a comforting hand on her shoulder, raised it to cup her face.

She closed her eyes, and for just a second, he thought she might have pressed her cheek against his palm, but the sensation was so fleeting, he couldn't be sure. By the time she opened her eyes again, she was back to her stoic, if somber, self.

"I know I deserve every sarcastic comeback brewing in your mind right now after my hard stance on hockey players and not going to your game, but do me a solid and save them for later? I just want to pay for my books and get out of here."

"Yeah, sure. My treat."

She smiled in thanks, and that fragility he'd glimpsed earlier shimmered around her again.

They drove back to the hotel in silence, and when he parked in front of the door, Lainey was frowning at her phone.

"What's the matter?"

"Nothing," she said, then relented at Cooper's dubious expression. "My Realtor just texted to say the guy who was supposed to tour the bar this morning never showed."

"That sucks. How come?"

"She doesn't know. He's not answering his phone now."

"It happens. Business deals fall through."

Lainey locked her screen before tucking the phone back in her purse. "It's starting to feel like I'm doomed to own this dive in perpetuity. The Drunken Sportsman is my purgatory."

Cooper quirked an eyebrow at her melodramatic summation. "Real estate is a long game, not a short con. Give it some time."

Lainey leaned back in the leather bucket seat, dragging a finger down the spines of the textbooks in her lap. "So you're a hockey star and a real estate mogul, huh?" She sat up a little straighter, and her pretty eyes sparked with renewed hope. "Any tips?"

She wanted his help.

Shit.

He'd been teasing her and now she was asking for advice. Deep-seated insecurity reared up and threatened to smother him. It took a very conscious effort for Cooper to remind himself that all the oxygen had not been sucked out of the world, and that he just had to breathe. He inhaled slowly through his nose, the way he used to do in school while he endured the angst-soaked moment as he waited for the teacher to decide which sacrificial lamb was going to be the next to read aloud from the textbook or solve a math problem on the board.

He'd made a massive tactical error and let his guard down, and now she was asking him questions in the false belief that he was even half as smart as she was. And since her earlier acknowledgment that she had a business degree, he knew the percentage was much lower than that.

He wasn't about to tell her that he had no plans for after he retired from hockey. No investments. No property. No passive income. The end of his career had always felt so far in the future, and it had taken so much effort to keep his issues with reading a secret from his agent that he'd never gotten around to hiring a business manager.

This was the very reason Cooper lived his social life in the currency of whirlwind flings and one-night stands with women who wanted to keep things as uncomplicated as he did.

He liked Lainey, but she hadn't needed to worry this morning when he'd stupidly invited her to watch a game. He could never venture into relationship territory with her. She was too smart. Too driven. He couldn't even keep up with this conversation, and she sure as hell wasn't impressed by his career. What could he possibly offer her?

"Well, I'm just a dumb hockey player, but I highly recommend hiring a guy. You get stuff like this taken care of, and you keep your hands clean. I always try to keep as many layers between me and the actual money as possible."

Her eyes darkened for a minute, as though a cloud had drifted through their gray-blue depths, and then cleared again. "Smart plan, Slick. You never know where that money has been."

He smiled, relieved that she'd followed his lead.

At least that was what he told himself after she'd said goodbye and crawled out of the Maserati. With a quick check in his rearview mirror, Cooper backed out and pointed his car toward home.

ONCE PLAYOFFS STARTED, Lainey didn't see much of Cooper. The team had a curfew, a strictly regimented practice schedule and a lot of interviews. Despite that, his legacy at the bar certainly lived on.

In the week since he'd body-checked his way into her life and made The Drunken Sportsman semifamous, there was a noticeable upswing in the profit column. Sports fans, hockey fans and Cooper Mead fans alike were stopping by to check out the place.

There was also, much to Darius's chagrin, a spike in Black Widow sales. Word had gotten out about the "secret menu item"—Lainey supposed she had Cooper's "date" to thank for that—and people were shelling out fifty bucks a pop to try one for themselves.

In keeping with liquor laws, and in the interest of increasing the profit margin, Lainey decided to keep the price but downsize the drink to a shot glass. Within the week, it had become all the rage to have your friends take a photo after you took the shot so you could compare your stank face to Cooper's.

And still, no serious offers on the bar were coming in. Jeannie, the Realtor, said she was getting lots of interested calls as the bar's profile rose, but for some reason, no one was taking that final step.

When she'd inherited the bar, Lainey had planned to be rid of it within two weeks of Martin's funeral. Then she'd seen the place, and it had become apparent how much work she'd need to do if she was going to turn a decent profit.

She'd cashed in a few of her investments to bring the kitchen up to code and fix the plumbing issues that had threatened to turn the men's bathroom into a sinkhole.

She'd spent the rest of the time implementing cosmetic changes—replacing cracked tiles, upgrading the bathroom counters, refreshing the glassware—that she believed were all that stood between her and getting the hell out of Portland.

It was a good property with a lot of potential. That's what the Realtor had told her.

But now, months later, it was hard to remain optimistic about her speedy timeline.

Don't give up, she chided herself, pulling on the white tank, dark-wash skinny jeans and black combat boots she favored for shifts at the bar. After a quick mirror check to make sure her teeth were lipstick-free, she tightened her ponytail and checked the time. Her bar shift started in twenty minutes.

Resolve stiffened her spine as she grabbed her jacket and headed for the door. Her dad owed her this. He hadn't bothered to be a father while he was alive. But for some reason that was beyond her, he'd left her this bar, and she wasn't going anywhere until she got what she was owed. She would do whatever it took to sell this bar and be free of Martin Sillinger's shadow once and for all.

LAINEY DROPPED HER purse on the counter and tried to process the melee before her. The Sportsman was packed to capacity with not just the regulars, but also a glittery, surgically enhanced club crowd that had no business in a sports bar. Never mind that it was only nine o'clock and there was already a rowdy lineup that snaked around the block. A couple of men she didn't recognize were playing bouncer, checking IDs and keeping the sequined mob inside down to numbers that almost complied with fire-safety regulations. A couple more strangers were unpacking large amounts of equipment on the tiny makeshift stage in the far corner.

"And get some more pineapple juice. No! *Pine. Apple. Juice.*" Darius's voice rose above the din, and Lainey turned to find him shouting into the phone. "I don't know! Apparently, people who wear a lot of rhinestones like to drink it with alcohol. And don't forget the cherries. We're almost out." Darius had barely hung up when he rounded and tossed an apron at her. "Where the hell have you been? You're late!"

"Traffic was unbelievable, and then I had to park two blocks away and fight my way through hordes of pedestrians. What the hell is going on here?"

"Your boyfriend scored the winning goal tonight, and the Storm swept Wyoming in four games straight. Playoff fever has officially taken over Portland." Darius flicked a glance in her direction even as he began pouring what Lainey guessed would end up a Long Island iced tea. "So now Geoff and Raj are doing their best to keep your bar legal. Malcolm's helping his brother set up his DJ stuff because your jukebox is a piece of crap, and I have packs of Kappas roaming grocery stores and liquor barns for all the crazy shit girls in spandex like to drink. In short, my frat brothers are saving your ass, and you owe me big time. Pass me another box of…" The request was lost in the clamor.

"What?"

"Straws!"

Lainey complied automatically, staring in awe as people jostled for Darius's attention. Her bar was busy. Her bar was crazy busy. The slightest hint of a smile pulled at her mouth. There was no way she wouldn't have the bar sold soon if this kept up.

Then a storm cloud in the form of Aggie Demille trundled up to the bar and rained all over Lainey's sequin-wearing, cash-wielding parade. "Well, don't just stand there gawkin' with your purse takin' up valuable counter space. Put on that apron and pour me some Cosmopolitans for the prissy missies at table fourteen."

"Cosmopolitans?" Lainey asked, shoving her purse under the counter with a frown. *Sex and the City* had been off the air for more than a decade. Did people still drink Cosmos?

"Yeah, five of 'em. And put a rush on it." Aggie exchanged a tray full of empty shooter glasses for both of Darius's newly completed Long Island iced teas before she pushed her way back into the gyrating mass. Until last week, the Sportsman's usual clientele had thought pouring a bottle of beer into a glass was too fancy. Apparently the pierced and spangled had a more refined sense of the frou-frou.

Lainey leaned toward Darius, who was assembling a couple of shooters. "What the hell is in a Cosmopolitan?"

He pushed a tattered bartending guide toward her. "Page forty-three." Darius topped off the shooter with a squirt of aerated edible oil product. "And for the record, I'd just like to take this opportunity to apologize on behalf of my gender's preoccupation with this particular sexual act, because I swear to you, Lainey, if one more person asks me for a Blow Job, I'm going to lose it."

"Preaching to the choir, my brother. Welcome to the plight of straight women everywhere."

Aggie pushed her way back up to the counter. "I'm gonna need two Gladiators, a Monkey's Lunch, a Black Widow and three more Blow Jobs. And be quick about it, Darius. We don't have time for you to be an artist with the whipped cream."

Darius's jaw tightened at the jab. "Is a little appreciation too much to ask for?"

Lainey gave him a reassuring pat on the back. "Aw, just ignore her, Darius. I'm sure you give good head."

He snagged the can of whipped cream off the counter with undue force and Lainey smiled as she leafed through the sticky guide in search of page forty-three.

9

HE'D LEFT THE state for four days, played two hockey games and scored a goal with a beauty of a slap shot to send the Storm into the second round of the playoffs, and all Cooper could think about was getting back to Portland. Getting back to Lainey.

Things had been a little strained between them since he'd dropped her off at her hotel that night when she'd been ambushed by her ex-teammate and he'd been so flippant about her business questions. He'd faked his way through, just as he always did in situations where he was out of his depth. They were his survival tactics, but with Lainey, they felt more like lies.

He was determined to set things right. If she'd let him. That was the unknown factor, and his stomach churned with nerves as he raised his fist to knock on her door. Why the hell had he chosen a dress shirt and black pants for their reunion? He probably looked like he was trying too hard.

"Cooper? What are you doing here?"

It was good to see her. Good enough that he tried to ignore the awkwardness of her greeting, like he was an old friend she wasn't sure she wanted to see. "They were expecting lightning, so the charter company moved up our flight time." He glanced past her at her new room on the second floor. It was smaller, more utilitarian. At least a couple hundred bucks a night less than her last room. "Were you going to tell me you moved, or just sneak out of town without a goodbye?"

The quick dart of her eyes to the carpet let him know the latter *had* crossed her mind.

"Turns out when the assignment is over, so's the premium room. But I decided to give it a few more weeks. Zenith's not happy about it, but they relented when I played the dead dad card. I'm just hoping I can unload the Sportsman before I run out of vacation days and hotel reward points. And I was going to text you about it once I was all settled. I *was*," she insisted, reading the doubt on his face.

"I wish you had. The elderly couple who are staying in your old room think I'm a crazy person now."

Lainey leaned against the door frame and crossed her arms. "So how did you find me?"

"I have my ways," he said, overly suavely, but instead of the laugh he'd been going for, she gave him a look that said, "Cut the shit," and he was the one who laughed.

Lainey was the whole package. Strong, smart and sarcastic as fuck. Cooper wondered how long it had been since he'd last genuinely liked a woman the way he liked her. And in deference to that, he confessed. "I let the desk clerk take a selfie with me."

"Glad to know my privacy is absolutely secure...unless a famous athlete wants to murder me. He's lucky I already submitted my report."

Cooper shrugged. "Well, in his defense, I'm *really*

good at hockey, so…it's not like he sold you out for a photo of a professional bowler or something. Your death will be honorable."

Her quick answering smile was too much to resist and he reached for her, his fingers circling her wrist. She swallowed, eyes darkening as she uncrossed her arms and allowed him to take her hand in his. Cooper ran his thumb down the middle of her palm. He took a small step toward her, even though he hadn't meant to. Magnetism, he supposed.

"Listen, Lainey. I know things have been a little… strained since the last time we saw each other, and I was hoping…" Cooper took a deep breath. "Can we go somewhere and talk?"

There was a long pause, and he wasn't quite sure which way she was going to go.

"I'm not exactly dressed for a date," she countered, looking down at her casual gray dress made of T-shirt material, then at his outfit.

"Not a date," he assured her.

"I'll put on some shoes."

His sigh was one of relief.

They ended up in a round booth at the back of a trendy taqueria.

The place was heavy on the hipsters, but there was a pretty good variety of people in the eclectically decorated restaurant that was a mix of weathered wood, intricate Aztec carvings, bright sugar skull prints and candles melting in Corona bottles to compensate for the dim overhead lighting. It was one of those places that had just the right ambience to make you feel like you were alone in the crowd.

It had been his agent's suggestion—Jared had been on Coop's back lately about not getting out enough, and when Cooper had told him about his meeting Marty Sillinger's daughter, Golden had suggested he take her somewhere nice.

Lainey grabbed her menu while he set his phone and keys on the table.

"You already know what you want?" Lainey slid a couple of degrees closer on the bench seat, ostensibly so he could hear her over the background noise, but he liked to think she wasn't unaware that it upped the intimacy.

"No. I like to hear what the server recommends," he explained, relying as always on the coping mechanism that had got him through countless meals in countless restaurants.

"Sounds like you spend a lot of money paying for things you don't want to eat," she teased.

"I like to be adventurous."

He moved his leg, and his knee came to rest against hers.

She raised her eyes from the menu at the contact, but she didn't pull away.

"Hi, I'm Tiffany and I'll be your server tonight. Can I grab you anything to drink?"

Lainey started at the server's sudden intrusion.

"I think two Coronas and two waters?" Coop said, waiting for Lainey's quick head bob of confirmation before he turned his attention to the young woman dressed in a black T-shirt, black jeans and black Chucks, her stoplight-red hair done in an old-timey style that wouldn't have looked out of place in the 1950s.

"Sounds good. I'll be back in a minute to take your order."

"This is a nice place."

"I can't stop thinking about you."

She seemed to sober as the intensity of his words registered.

"I'm in the middle of the biggest playoff run of my career and I can't focus."

"Cooper..."

His phone rang, and he glanced at the screen. Since it was the worst possible moment, he wasn't surprised to see the identity of the caller. "It's your brother."

"Go ahead and answer. I'm going to use the ladies' room. Order me the chicken tacos if she comes by while I'm gone. Extra guac."

Coop answered the phone as she left.

"What do you want, Rookie? I'm kind of in the middle of something here."

"*Sports Nation* published this article about me, and it's full of lies!"

"Come on, man, I told you not to set that Google alert. And as for the article, that's part of the job. Don't let them get in your head."

"They're saying I have the worst plus/minus on the team and that I'm too young and I'm not ready for the pressure of being in the playoffs!"

Cooper remembered Danny's assessment. "You *do* have the worst plus/minus on the team."

"Well, thanks for nothing. Some mentor you are."

Tiffany appeared beside him and dropped off their drinks and a basket of chips and salsa. Coop covered the mouthpiece and asked for two orders of chicken tacos, one with extra chicken, and a side of guacamole before he returned his attention to Brett.

"Look, you want some advice? Get off the internet

for a couple of days. TV, too. Go work out, play some video games and get some sleep. It doesn't matter what they say. It matters what you do. If you want to stick it to them, play better next time."

Brett relented with a sigh. "I guess you're right. We still on for breakfast on Thursday? Before practice?"

"Yeah. Sure. I guess. But only if you do what I tell you."

"Hey, Coop? Before you go…did you have any play-off tickets for the next round that you were looking to get rid of? I already gave mine away, but I could use another set."

"I'll have to get back to you on that. I'm hoping one of the kids from the hospital can use mine, but we're still figuring out the logistics." Danny's mom was trying to clear it with the doctors, make sure they okayed it before getting Danny's hopes up.

"Okay, let me know if you have extras. I'll take whatever you've got left. See you Thursday."

"What did he want?" Lainey asked, sliding back into the booth.

Cooper set the phone back on the table. "Advice. Hockey tickets. Food. Has he always been so damn needy?"

"I…don't know."

Cooper was surprised by the revelation, but even more so by the fact that she seemed just as surprised. "I…well, except for the funeral and all the lawyer stuff that happened with the will, the last time I saw Brett was when he was seven."

Cooper had spent his share of time sitting at poker tables, but judging by her scowl, he obviously needed to work on his poker face.

"My dad was an asshole. He left us, me and my mom. Walked right out the day after my tenth birthday, and you know what he said to me? 'Later, kiddo.' That's it. And then I didn't see him again until he and his shiny new family came by because, 'Brett should get to know his sister.' I mean, were they serious?

"My mom cried for a week after that visit. And a week after that, we moved to LA. To 'start fresh,' she said. After that, I didn't see them again until my mom died."

Coop moved his hand to cover hers on the table, silently urging her to go on.

"She was killed in a car accident on her way home from work when I was seventeen. I got shipped back to Portland to live with my dad and his new family while I finished my last semester of high school and counted down the days until I turned eighteen and could head out on my own.

"I spent six months in their house, with this annoying little kid who wouldn't leave me alone. 'C'mon, Elaine! Let's play street hockey. Wanna play video games? Will you take me to the store to buy some candy?' He was always right there. Bugging me."

The heat left her words somewhere in the middle, as her adult self recognized what her grieving, teenage self hadn't. Lainey dropped her eyes, and Cooper recognized her shame, because he felt it, too. A twinge of recognition deep in his chest. *Will you help me with my slap shot? Wanna grab a drink? What was your first year in the league like?* Grown-up equivalents from someone who wanted desperately to fit in.

Fucking Sillinger, he thought, but all of the heat was self-directed.

"Sounds like he wanted some company. And to get to know you a little better."

Lainey shrugged. "Yeah. I guess. I just… I hated him. Maybe not him, but what he represented. He was my dad's new kid. My replacement. He had two parents, and I didn't have anything anymore." Lainey swiped at her eye with the back of her hand, and Cooper didn't know what to do. He wanted to hold her, but she would hate that.

"I was a total asshole to him." Lainey's frown was back, and Cooper gave in to his need to touch her, placing his hand on her back. "And later, during my first year of college, when I found out that my dad had gotten divorced again, I was glad. I was glad Brett had to go through what I went through. Had to feel the same pain I felt. That's so awful. So vindictive."

"Hey. You were a kid yourself. And you'd just lost your mom. And you had every right to be mad at your dad. You can't be so hard on yourself. You were doing the best you could."

She was so sad, and Cooper felt like a bit of an ass at the pleasure he took when she tucked herself under his arm, and dropped her forehead on his shoulder. "I shouldn't have taken it out on Brett. He was seven. He didn't do anything wrong."

"Hey, seven-year-olds can be total bastards. I speak from experience."

The words were out of Cooper's mouth before he'd thought them through—a truth meant to soothe her guilt, at least a little, but also an unintended glimpse into one of the worst years of his childhood. He didn't want to talk about it, was usually careful not to bring it up.

"I'll bet. You were a real hell-raiser, huh?"

Cooper tried not to be hurt that she assumed he was talking about having been a bully, when he was the one who'd been mercilessly picked on back then. But it was better than her knowing why he'd been the target…at least until he'd hit a growth spurt in junior high, and cool stopped being about what happened in the classroom and started being about clothes and sports and girls. That was when he'd figured out that fitting in was about putting on a good show. And he'd been performing ever since.

Which was the reason he shot her a cocky smile. "You know it. Ladies love it when you've got a bit of the devil in you."

She straightened up, using the lifeline he'd thrown to find her way out of their earlier conversation, putting herself back together right in front of his eyes. "Oh, ladies do, do they?"

Cooper shifted his hand from her shoulders to the back of the bench, respecting her show of strength but unwilling to move too far from her. "Haven't heard you complaining."

"Then you haven't been listening very hard."

"Sorry, what did you say?"

Lainey rolled her eyes at the bad joke, reaching for her beer.

"I'm serious! I was very distracted. I don't know if you know this, but I find a woman drinking a longneck intensely erotic. I've always had a thing for smokin' hot women who have a bit of that 'one of the guys' mentality."

Lainey smiled and leaned closer to him.

"I don't think that's the reason you like it so much," she countered, her voice pitched low enough that he leaned a bit closer in response.

"Oh, no?"

She shook her head, biting her lip as she squeezed the lime into the bottle with her thumb. She licked the citrus from her thumb, and Cooper might have groaned, but he couldn't be sure.

"You want to know what I think it is?"

Cooper managed a nod.

Lainey made him wait for it, wrapping her fingers around the Corona with deliberate precision before bringing the beer to her lips for a long pull.

His gaze never left her mouth as she lowered the bottle and licked her lips.

Cooper set his jaw against the sudden hunger in his belly. Hunger that had nothing to do with tacos.

"I think it's because men are easily turned on by penis metaphors," she finished, quirking a brow as she drew the pad of her thumb across her bottom lip.

Judging by the effect her calculated seduction was having on a certain part of his anatomy, he was in no position to dispute her theory. "So what do you think, Slick? Am I right?"

"About me being turned on? Definitely."

Their server chose that auspicious moment to show up and announce, "Here are your chicken tacos, one with extra meat."

"Tiffany, your timing could not be better. We were just discussing the merits of extra meat, weren't we, Lainey?"

His comment startled a laugh from Lainey, but Tiffany remained unflappable.

"Whatever. Here's your side of guac. Enjoy."

"You are a twelve-year-old boy," Lainey admonished, digging into her tacos.

"I really am."

"I think Tiffany there is the first woman I've seen who would definitely not sleep with you."

"Luckily for me, she's not the woman I was hoping to impress."

Lainey gave him a playful scowl. "I thought we agreed this wasn't a date."

"Well, that's a relief. Because if was a date, it would be going really well."

"You think?"

"Oh, definitely. Good food, cold beer, dirty jokes, sexual tension. If this was a date, I'd definitely be getting lucky tonight."

"I know you think this Mr. Charming routine is going to make me change my mind, but you're still not getting in my pants."

"Lucky for me, you're not wearing pants, so I can hold out hope."

"Eat your tacos."

Cooper smiled and followed orders.

THEIR LEVEL OF the parkade was completely deserted when they spilled out of the elevator, laughing. Lainey's footsteps echoed in the cavernous concrete structure, the hard soles of her sandals in direct contrast to Cooper's stealthier suede boots.

The Maserati was parked on an angle near a pillar on the far end of the structure, the buzzing light illuminating the side closest to them, leaving the far side of the vehicle in shadow.

"I feel like we're in a car commercial." She looked over at Cooper—dark good looks, stylishly messy hair, black dress shirt open at the collar, cuffs rolled up his forearms—and amended her statement. "Or a music video."

"I'm surprised it's so dead up here. Especially since the restaurant was so busy."

"It's Tuesday night," Lainey offered by way of explanation.

"In New York, that's no excuse."

"It's not in LA, either. But I kind of like cities that don't try quite so hard. Sometimes the bustle is overwhelming. It's easier to get lost in, but that can make it hard to find yourself."

Cooper nodded thoughtfully. "I didn't know you were such a philosopher. So, are you trying to get lost or get found?"

The sudden depth of the conversation made Lainey feel like she was drowning. "I'm just here for the tacos."

"Hey, nothing wrong with tacos," he agreed, letting her off the hook, although the look on his handsome face let her know that she hadn't escaped; he'd let her get away.

They walked in silence, except for steady slap of her sandals, their hands still clasped, and Lainey leaned her head against his broad shoulder. Her free hand came across her body so she could trace her fingers down the ink that swirled across his forearms.

"I had fun tonight," she confessed, but in the echo chamber of the parking garage, it came out louder than she'd intended. Or maybe it only felt loud because she meant it so much.

Cooper's hand tightened in hers as they approached the car.

She'd thought he'd meant it in an encouraging, "me, too" kind of way as he walked her to the passenger door, but when she glanced up, it wasn't to find the easy smile she expected. He looked dangerous, bathed in shadows, like the kind of guy mothers warned their daughters about.

"The night's not over."

The simple words laden with so much meaning made her mouth go dry.

He let go of her hand and ran his knuckles up her arm, from wrist to elbow, then higher and higher still until he encountered the strap of her dress. He tugged it down baring her shoulder, and dipped his head to kiss the spot he'd revealed. Lainey's head fell back, rewarding Cooper with unfettered access, and he took advantage, kissing the pulse point at the base of her neck, his playoff stubble scraping the tender skin.

"That tickles," she breathed as her cheek came to rest against his ear. He kissed and licked his way up her throat, nipped the sensitive skin behind her ear. "Tell me to stop."

"Not yet."

Cooper grabbed her hips, his grip biting into her skin through the thin material of her dress, and she shivered despite the heat. Aching for him. Her body strained for his touch, and a warm rush of tingling heat settled at the apex of her thighs. Her skin was a magnet, so desperate to be pressed against his that she could feel herself swaying close, closer, but thanks to the barrier of their clothes, not close enough.

"I want you. I want on top of you, inside you, all of you."

Lainey bit her bottom lip, entranced by the rough declaration, the baritone of his voice rumbling through her chest, through every part of her.

He groaned. "Your mouth makes me want to do dirty things to you."

Her smile was feral, and she watched in fascination as his Adam's apple bobbed when he swallowed. "Jesus, Lainey. Don't look at me like that." His fingers flexed against her hips in warning, biting into her skin, and his body grew rigid—his biceps, his shoulders, his pecs. Even the set of his jaw.

"Like what?" she teased, cocking an eyebrow, issuing a challenge.

"Like you want me to fuck you right here."

She could see it, his full-body battle for control. She could smell the promise of high voltage in the air, like ozone before a thunderstorm. It made her breath come faster. "Maybe I do."

That lightning strike she'd been anticipating flashed in his eyes. He took a predatory step forward, forced her back against the car. The heat of him made her melt, but the sudden shock of cool metal and glass against her bare back turned her sigh into a gasp.

He cursed, almost reverently, and dropped his forehead against hers. She could feel him wrestling for control. "Someone might see us."

He was trying to be a gentleman, she knew, but the gesture was wholly unnecessary, and to prove it Lainey reached between them, reveling in his sharp intake of breath as she tugged his belt loose. "Then we'd better hurry." She lifted her head, felt his shaky exhalation against her mouth, and bit his bottom lip.

His hands tunneled through her hair, bracing her head as he covered her lips with his, working her mouth with such focused desperation that she thought she might die of pleasure. Then he wedged a leg between hers and her dress rode up until his thigh pressed intimately between her legs and she decided there was no better way to go.

Lainey redoubled her efforts on his belt, desperate to get to the button on his pants, but her clumsy hands fumbled as he kissed her inside out, licking into her mouth, and distracting her with the sweet friction of his thigh against the barrier of her underwear.

With all the strength she possessed, Lainey pulled her mouth from his and went on offense, spinning him so that their positions were reversed.

He raised his eyebrows as she shoved him back against the Maserati. She had him unbuckled, unbuttoned and unzipped in seconds. "I told you I wanted you fast," she reminded him. "Now undo your shirt."

Cooper pinned her with smoldering brown eyes, as he began undoing buttons, every movement of his fingers revealing a little more of his chest to her hungry gaze.

"Your turn." The challenge in his voice turned her on even more.

Lainey shimmied her panties down her thighs. "You've got a condom, right?"

She stood up to find him ripping into a square of foil. She didn't analyze how much of her smile was directly attributable to relief, but she knew it was a lot. "Didn't know you were such a Boy Scout."

Cooper glanced up from the task of sheathing himself. "I wasn't. Dropped out when I discovered there's not actually a badge for condom preparedness. Had to strike out on my own to earn those credentials."

She licked her lips as he reached for her, pulled her close. "How industrious of you."

He tugged her dress up her thighs. "You haven't seen anything yet."

Lainey was deliciously light-headed with arousal and danger. She'd never strayed out of the bedroom before, but she understood the appeal now. There was something so hot about the buzz of fluorescent lights, the scent of concrete and gasoline, and the risk of getting caught. Cooper wasn't even inside her yet, and she was already so turned on that her orgasm felt imminent, pulsing so close to the surface that for once, coming seemed like a "when", not an "if."

Then Cooper grabbed her by the backs of her thighs and pulled her up to his body, swallowing her cry of surprise with his kiss as she wrapped her legs around his waist and held on as he slid inside her body.

Cooper reversed their positions again, shoving her against the car, and she buried her face in the crook of his neck as he drove inside her again and again as Lainey whispered dirty words of encouragement. This wasn't about finesse, it was about fucking, and with every thrust, Lainey flew higher and higher. She buried her hand in his hair, tugging his head back and kissing him as she came, fast and hard, the sharp contractions of her body pulling him over the edge with her.

10

"Why are you smiling like that?"

Lainey looked up from the narrow swath of counter she'd been wiping for who knew how long before Darius's arrival.

"What? I'm not smiling like anything."

Certainly not like a woman who'd been fucked senseless against a car that was worth a cool two hundred grand. Besides, just because a woman had expanded her sexual repertoire and her list of turn-ons to include sex in a public parking garage didn't mean she smiled differently.

She shivered at the memory of Cooper's gravelly voice. *I want you. I want on top of you, inside you, all of you.* Everything about last night had been so damn hot.

"I'm serious, Lainey. Stop. It's creeping me out."

Lainey took a deep breath and schooled her features into her best boss persona. "Fine. But only because I need to talk to you for a second before you start."

She motioned toward the empty table near the window, and despite the odd look he gave her, Darius complied.

She followed him over, preparing herself for what she had to say as she took the seat across from him. This was going to be hard.

"I know you and I have an unusual working history."

The table started to jiggle as Darius bounced the heel of his red hightop against the floor.

"What's going on? Are you firing me? This is about the bottle of Crown that got broken the other night, isn't it? Because my frat will pay for it. It was so busy in here, and Geoff accidentally knocked it off the counter when—"

"Would you shut up for a second and let me thank you already?"

Clearly taken aback, Darius snapped his mouth shut. When her words finally registered, he shrugged, modest for the first time since she'd met him. "Don't mention it."

"I wish I didn't have to," she admitted, startling a smile from her barkeep. "But we're kind of a team here, and you stepped up, rallying your frat brothers like that. You saved the day. You did. And I appreciate it."

"It's no big deal. You're not so bad," he relented, and it was Lainey's turn to smile. "I mean, I know getting saddled with this place wasn't what you were expecting. And that there's a complicated history to it. I've got a dad, too. I know how it can be."

Lainey's lips twisted at his assessment. *Complicated* seemed too bland a word to describe her relationship with Martin Sillinger. "I doubt that."

"No, I definitely have a dad. I mean, I can bring in a family photo if you want."

She rolled her eyes. "Ha ha. I know you have a dad. One who's incredibly proud of you, I'll bet. You're going to be a lawyer. You're doing the family proud. Well, I

mean, you would be if you shaved off that awful goatee."
Lainey couldn't help but slide in the jibe.

Now it was Darius's turn to roll his eyes.

"My brother—" Lainey frowned, paused. The word
had come out so quickly, so naturally, that it startled her.
She'd never called Brett her brother before. It usually
grated just to hear other people say it.

"He plays hockey professionally. He made it to the big
show and Martin could barely make the effort to con-
gratulate him. What chance did I have?"

Darius sighed. "Look, Lainey. The truth is, I didn't
know Martin that well. Obviously, I know nothing about
what kind of dad he was. But let me show you something."

"You know I'll have to fire you on the spot if you ex-
pose yourself to me."

Darius stood as he shot her a withering glare. "You
have a gift for fucking up nice moments, you know that,
right?"

Lainey curtseyed when she got to her feet, but followed Darius past the bar and around to the hallway by
the bathrooms. He stopped at the photo wall, and Lainey
braced herself before she followed his gaze.

She hated the wall. Had since the first time she'd
walked into the bar.

She didn't want to look at smiling photos of her father
throughout the years.

The ones where he was younger reminded her of the
good times—birthday cakes and hockey practices—all
the things they'd done before the drinking had gotten
bad and the fighting had started. The ones where he was
older, when he was all but a stranger to her, were pain-
ful in a different way. She'd taken to keeping her eyes

down when she needed to get cleaning supplies or use the bathroom.

But today she made herself look.

"The day I got hired, Martin brought me back here and pointed out three photos to me. The first one was the one of him meeting Wayne Gretzky."

Lainey rolled her eyes, a bitter laugh escaping. "His pride and joy."

"The second," Darius continued, "was him and your brother the night Brett got drafted by the Storm."

Lainey looked at the photo, realized she never had before. She was struck by two things. The first was how incredibly young Brett looked. It was a lot, to achieve your dreams at eighteen. A lot to handle. A lot of chances for things to go badly if you didn't have anyone around.

The second was that, while Martin was beaming at the camera, Brett's attention was on Martin. Even in that moment, probably the greatest moment of his young life, Brett still couldn't fully enjoy it without approval from the man beside him.

"And the third was that one up there."

Lainey followed the direction of his finger to find a framed, yellowing newspaper article that she recognized. Speaking of looking like a kid…the photo had that slightly blurry look of black-and-white newsprint, but she looked young and intense in her US jersey. The headline read "Local Hockey Player Makes National Squad."

She bit her lip, concentrating on the pain. She'd had no idea she'd made Martin's wall of fame. And though she fought it, there was a warm spot in her heart. He'd cared. At least a little. At least for a moment.

"I'm not saying that Martin was father of the year. But he was still your dad."

She nodded. He was her dad. And while this small gesture wasn't enough to untangle her thorny feelings about her family history, it did make her realize one thing. She wasn't that different from Brett after all, because she, too, craved the approval of the man who'd raised her, at least for the first ten years of her life.

"You liked him, huh?"

"Martin? Yeah. He was a good guy. Customers liked him. Always quick with a smile or an opinion about sports. Way more go-with-the-flow than you," Darius said pointedly as they headed back to the bar.

"So much for our truce."

"Please don't tell me that because I was nice to you once, I have to be nice to you all the time now, because if that's the case, fire me and put me out of my misery."

"Actually, I was trying to figure out what it would take to get you to quit. I'll be keeping the 'force you to be nice to me' card in my pocket for the future," Lainey assured him. "Now go get your apron on and get to work. The bar opens in twenty minutes and I'm not paying you to stand around."

They shared a smile as Darius got to work, but Lainey's grin faded as she glanced around the Sportsman. Usually when she thought of her dad, his life after he left her... there was so much hurt and pain wrapped around it.

Now things looked different.

Martin Sillinger had been a person, with a business that was doing okay, staff who kinda liked him, customers who kinda missed him. He'd been the villain to her for so long that this abrupt shift in perspective gave her vertigo.

He was just a man who'd lost his hockey career to an

injury and had struggled to fill the hole. If anyone could empathize with that, it should be her.

Much as she hated to admit it, maybe Martin had built something good here. There was a sense of community she hadn't expected at all.

Ever since she'd left Portland for good, there'd been a piece of her, an agitated, furtive piece, that was always looking over her shoulder, always on edge. That part of her had quieted since she'd been back. She didn't feel as lost anymore. And she liked it.

SINCE THEIR HEART-TO-HEART, Lainey and Darius were all work and no insults. She figured they'd get back to normal once the awkwardness had passed but in the meantime, the night was going smoothly. Game time was in an hour, so they'd put the pregame shows on the TV, and the bar was starting to fill up with fans eager to see who the Storm would be playing in the next round.

When a tall man wearing a ball cap over his dark hair walked through the door, face shadowed with heavy stubble and hands shoved in the pockets of his black field jacket, Lainey wasn't fooled by his attempt at anonymity. Cooper tucked his big frame into an empty table in the corner of the bar and returned Lainey's smile when their eyes met. Anticipating his order, she grabbed a glass of ice water and headed over.

She was almost there, her smile growing with every step, when the sound of her name on the television froze her to the spot.

"In case you haven't read *Sports Nation*'s latest headline, they broke the news earlier that Cooper Mead, PWR Athletics brand ambassador, is dating Elaine Sillinger, and if that name rings a bell, it should. Not only is she the half sister of Mead's fellow Portland Storm defenseman, Brett Sillinger, but you might also remember her from that time she scored on her own net and cost America a gold medal. So as the Storm advance in the playoffs, let's hope, for Mead's sake, that tendency isn't contagious."

The world stopped as Lainey glanced up at the television. The footage felt unnecessary—it was already burned into her brain. She didn't need to see it to know exactly what was about to happen.

She stood facing her goalie on the right side of the net, number 42 emblazoned on her American jersey as she watched her defensive partner fight for the puck behind the net. The girl on the Canadian team won the battle, flicked the puck out in front of the net and Lainey got her stick on it. Even now, she didn't know why she'd rushed, why she hadn't angled her body more, why she hadn't backhanded it out of the zone instead. For some reason that remained a mystery to her no matter how many times she'd relived this moment, a combination of adrenaline, nerves and bad aim had conspired when she'd shot the puck, and instead of banking it off the boards and behind the net the way she'd intended, it flew straight into the bottom corner, putting the Canadians ahead by a goal with forty-three seconds left on the clock.

Everything went hot, her skin tingling as though her body were trying to spontaneously combust, but she'd screwed that up, too, and now she stood there, awash in a fire that wouldn't take. She was unaware that the glass had tumbled out of her hand, but the spray of cold water against her feet and the crash of the glass shattering across the floor registered distantly, as though she'd watched it happen to someone else.

She hurt. Her whole body, her whole being, ached with

that familiar throb of acute shame—the one she'd spent three years trying to numb. But all this time, it had just been bubbling under the surface, churning and roiling like lava in a volcano that was just waiting to erupt. And erupt it had, leaving the emotional equivalent of Pompeii in its wake.

This was the moment her nightmares were about. This was the moment she'd dreaded since *the goal that shook America.*

"Turn it off. Dammit, turn it off!" Cooper's voice echoed in her brain, and then he was there, arms around her, and his touch pulled her back to the present. She could feel people's eyes on her, hear the din of whispered voices as the bar patrons put the footage and her reaction together, shared their findings with their tablemates.

"No. It's game night. Leave it. I just… I need to get out of here. I need to go home."

Aggie was already rushing over with a broom when Cooper put a hand on Lainey's back and guided her into the short hallway that led to the staff exit, which was good, because despite her declaration, she was having a hard time moving.

"Lainey—"

"It's fine. I'm fine. It's in the past. Or at least it was." She gestured behind her, toward the site of her latest humiliation, the image of her, standing alone and dejected in a crowd of players around the American net, still burned onto the screen of her mind.

Lainey buried her face in her hands even though she was far too hollow for any tears to come out. Like a fool, she'd let herself open up again, make friends, joke with patrons and banter with staff.

This was the price of being close to people. Eventually, you'd let them down.

She'd known Cooper meant trouble for her the second he walked up to the counter, but instead of shutting him down and remaining detached the way she should have, she'd flirted back. She'd opened up. And now her life was a burning pile of wreckage again. Everything she'd built back up was smoldering around her feet.

Because she'd let him in. His fame was her downfall—she'd known it would be, but she'd gambled anyway. And lost.

He slid his arms around her, tried to comfort her, but she twisted out of his embrace. The hurt look on his handsome face was her penance. "Lainey, please…"

She shook her head, stopping his words. "This is why I brought breakfast back to the hotel. But then we went to the bookstore, and when you invited me for dinner… I knew I shouldn't have gone out with you." Lainey ducked into the small office and grabbed her purse, taking a moment to steel herself against Cooper's magnetic charm, reminding herself that not resisting him in the first place was the reason she was in this mess now.

"I don't want to live the life you live—cameras everywhere, pictures in the paper and the gossip blogs. I've been through this all before, and I can't do it again. The first time nearly broke me. I won't do it again, not even for you."

The tears she'd thought beyond her trailed down her cheeks as she whirled around and strode the final three steps of the hallway and escaped out into the parking lot.

11

COOPER FLICKED AIMLESSLY through channels, stretched out on his couch in sweats and a T-shirt, trying to distract himself. It wasn't working, because there was nothing on. But thanks to the playoff curfew, it was too late to go out, even if he'd felt like it. Which he didn't. Because the only place he wanted to be was the one place he couldn't go: with Lainey.

He couldn't get that goddamn television footage out of his head.

He'd seen it before, of course. It had been played incessantly after it had happened. *The goal that shook America.*

In fact, Cooper had been in Vancouver, but playing for Canada, and while he'd crossed paths with some of the women on the American team in the village and at the rink, Elaine Sillinger hadn't been on his radar. In fact, if he was honest, while he remembered the incident and the resulting media shit-storm, her name had never registered on his consciousness. He'd been focused on his team's performance, on his own stake in the games.

It was weird to think that something that had barely meant anything to him had left her life in shambles.

He knew, to a lesser extent, what it was to be haunted by the play that went wrong—he had a number of those himself, although none as burned into the national conscience as hers.

He wasn't sure when it had started, this need to make sure she was okay. But when he'd reached for her, intending to comfort her, she'd shaken him off. And the dismissal was a blow. Lainey certainly didn't want his comfort. Hell, she didn't want him at all.

Cooper flicked the television off and stared up at the ceiling of his living room. It was only 11:00 p.m., but he could already tell his insomnia would be in full force tonight.

The ring of his phone startled him, and he reached behind his head and over the arm of the couch to grab the device from the side table. A glance at the screen made him sigh. It was Golden. Of course it was.

"How's my favorite client? You are dominating the news cycle, my man."

"Yeah. I'm on top of the world." Cooper ran a hand through his hair with a bitter laugh. "They talked about my personal life on a hockey pregame show and identified me not by my team or my position, but as fucking 'brand ambassador' for PWR Athletics." He shook his head. "I mean, how did they even know Lainey and I…"

Cooper trailed off, feeling like a moron. He should have known. He should have fucking known. "You did this."

Golden didn't ask for clarification, and that was enough.

"You fucking traitor."

"What choice did you leave me? The meme tided them

over for a while, but some goddamn dive bar in Portland isn't the image PWR is going for. At least hooking up with a disgraced Olympian will get the gossip mags reprinting photos of your former relationships and remind people you used to hang out in the most exclusive clubs in New York."

Cooper couldn't believe what he was hearing. "I told you about Lainey as a friend. Don't you give a shit about anything but the bottom line?"

"We're not friends, Mead. We're business partners, and you weren't keeping your end of the bargain, so I did what I had to do. Because the bottom line is the only thing that matters to me. PWR drops you, it makes other sponsors start to question you, too. Do you get that, Mead? It's a ripple effect."

"Well, how's this for a ripple? You're fired."

Jared's bark of laughter was obnoxiously condescending. "You're not firing me."

"Actually, Golden, you're right. I'm not. First, I want you to tell PWR Athletics I'm done. And get me the fuck out of that Lone Wolf contract, too. Then you're fired."

There was silence on the line as Golden realized he was serious.

"You're not going to find a better agent than me. No one can make you the money I can. I hope your piece of ass was worth tens of millions, because that's what you're giving up if you fire me."

Cooper bolted upright on the couch, muscles coiled, hands fisted. "You say anything like that about Lainey ever again and I won't just fire you, I will end you, you son of a bitch."

He swore again as he hung up the phone. It took all his willpower to drop it on the couch instead of chucking it against the wall. Cooper ran his fingers through his hair and got to his feet. Jared Golden was an asshole of the highest order. Cooper knew it. He'd always known it. Jared had been the first agent to dangle promises of shiny things in front of his teenage eyes, and Coop had bitten, because the last thing he needed was a bunch of legalese that he couldn't read. He'd believed Jared Golden when he'd told him he couldn't do any better.

For the first time, he realized that he might've been wrong. Maybe he *could* do better. For Lainey's sake, he had to try.

Cooper paced the length of the room, trying to burn off the anger simmering in his body, the desperate need to punch something. But he was in the playoffs. Hockey was all-important right now. He couldn't afford to bust up his hand in a childish tantrum.

The phone rang less than ten minutes later, and Cooper's grin was feral. Maybe yelling at Golden some more would help him let off some steam.

But when he picked up the phone, caller ID confirmed it wasn't Jared. Instead, it was the last person he'd expected to hear from, and surprise drained some of the pent-up rage from his system.

"Lainey? What's—"

"Yeah, this guy at your door in the fancy suit won't let me up to see you because he says I'm not on the list."

Something about her voice wasn't quite right. It was too mellow, and the words ran together at the end. Cooper frowned. "Are you drunk?"

"I'm not drunk. I am tipsy. I've had a bad day, no dinner, and two and a half beers. Sue me. But first tell Pete here to let me out of lobby jail."

"Yeah, okay. Put him on." Cooper tried to digest the

circumstance at hand as he waited for Lainey to hand the phone to the night doorman. After a moment of muted shuffling and some muffled chatter he couldn't make out, a man cleared his throat on the other end of the line. "Hello?"

"Hey, Pete. It's Cooper Mead in the penthouse. Sorry about this, and thank you for dealing so professionally with the situation, but you can send her up."

"HE SAYS GO right up," Pete told her, handing back her phone.

Lainey was not gracious in victory, taking a swig of her third beer before she took his offering and shoved it in her pocket. "Told you so, Mr. Nobody-Goes-Up-There-Without-Permission."

The doorman remained unflappable, and simply directed her toward the bank of mirrored elevators with an impassive gaze. It was very unsatisfying, Lainey decided as she followed his directions through the swanky white marble foyer.

Cooper was standing at the elevator when the doors slid open.

"Please tell me you didn't drive here."

"I took an Uber. Because, as I said on the phone, I've had a couple of drinks. And I didn't want any stupid reporters following me."

Coop's gaze snapped to hers as they stepped into his apartment. "Reporters are following you?"

Lainey shook her head, then grabbed his arm to steady herself. "Not yet. But they will be now because I had to walk through a whole swarm of them to get into your building. Darius texted to let me know that they've already invaded the bar, like bloodsucking leeches...but for information instead of blood. Like information-sucking leeches. I hate reporters. A lot. I think I need to sit down."

"Yeah, that's not a bad idea," Coop agreed, grabbing the beer bottle from her grasp before helping her to the couch. "Let me get you some food."

Lainey grabbed her phone out of her pocket and pulled up the familiar photo of Cooper, his face twisted in pure disgust as he stared at the Black Widow she'd given him, and the words: TFW YOU FIND OUT YOUR GIRLFRIEND COST THE US A GOLD MEDAL.

"Did you see this?" she asked, shoving it in his direction when he reappeared beside the couch. He traded her the phone for a box of fish-shaped crackers.

"What's it say?" he asked.

"It says I'm a laughingstock. That's what it says. Today is the worst." She popped the box open and ate a handful of the little orange crackers. They were pretty good, and they settled her stomach. She should have eaten dinner, but hurt and anger had stolen her appetite.

"Well, not *the* worst. Like, the fourth worst, but still."

He shot her a lopsided smile, like he didn't think she was being serious or something. "Well, if this is only fourth worst, I can't imagine how bad the *worst* was."

He was trying to lighten the mood, but in her slightly inebriated state, Lainey was too deep into the well of self-pity to grab the life preserver.

"The worst was *that* day. The one that was on the TV. I made a fool of myself. I scored on my own goaltender! And then I run into Shelly, and she's all, 'Why don't you come to the team reunions? It's so good to see you,' like everything's cool! I mean, what's wrong with her?"

Cooper sat down beside her and set her phone on the

glass coffee table. "Maybe she's moved on. Maybe the silver medal was enough for her."

"But that's worse, don't you see? It's worse if nobody cares about the thing that shaped me." She couldn't control the panic in her voice. "I let everyone down. My teammates. My country. My father."

Cooper shook his head. "I'm sure your dad was proud of you no matter—"

"He told me he wasn't. He came to Vancouver. I was so excited, because I'd finally gotten him to notice me. I'd finally made him proud. He hadn't been to one of my games in years, not since Brett was born, but he got on a plane for this game."

She laughed, because it was better than crying.

"And that's what happened. I screwed up in the most massive way a hockey player can. And you know what he said to me after? He said I was a disgrace to the Sillinger name. That I embarrassed him. And then he walked out of my life for the second time."

Lainey plunked the fish cracker box on the coffee table. Suddenly, she didn't feel very hungry. Or very drunk, for that matter. Certainly not drunk enough to be reliving this memory, but she couldn't make the words stop, now that they'd finally been let loose.

"I filed name change papers the day I got back. Harper is my mom's maiden name. I was going to change *Elaine*, too, but my mom named me after her mom, and I couldn't bring myself to break that connection with someone who actually loved me, so I left it and started going by Lainey instead."

She shook her head at her own stupidity. "I thought I could outrun it, that if I could just change who I was, keep moving, that this part of my life would be over. No more reporters and no more footage of my screwup on a constant loop."

"Jesus, Lainey. I wish to hell it worked that way. I'm so sorry you're going through this." Cooper placed a hand on her back.

It was warm and reassuring. It made her feel safe, and it made her remember the way the world melted away when she was wrapped in his arms. The way her brain went quiet, focused on nothing but pleasure when his hard body drove into hers. She craved that mindless release that only he could give her. Lainey put the crackers on the table beside her phone. "Maybe you can make it better." She slid closer to him, set her hand on his sweatpant-covered thigh.

"I don't think that's such a good idea."

"It's not like things can get any worse."

She leaned in closer. Moved her hand. "C'mon, Coop." His muscles jerked when she made contact with his stiffening cock. "I want you to make me feel good, make me writhe for you."

He jumped to his feet, and Lainey followed suit, anger clouding her vision and raising her voice. "God! What's your problem! I'm asking you to fuck me, not murder a bunch of puppies!"

"What the hell did you expect? You come here all riled up, angry at the world and you think some dirty words are going to change the fact that a few hours ago you dumped me? You wouldn't even let me hug you! And now you're sad and you want to fuck and I'm supposed to say thank-you?"

It was like he'd slapped her. The sting of rejection made her skin burn.

"What, you want to 'make love'?" She spat the words

with derision. "Cuddle all night? Pretend to make this more than it is?"

"Jesus, Lainey. I'm thirty-two years old. That's way too old to be dealing with this garbage. You had a shitty day. And your dad was an asshole, and I'm sorry. And I'm even more sorry that I'm indirectly responsible for bringing it all out in the open again. But you're not drunk enough to believe this is going to solve anything."

"I can't believe you're complaining that I want to escape with some hot sex."

"I'm not eighteen anymore. Hot isn't enough." He raked a hand down his face. "What are we even doing here, Lainey? Are we fooling around? Are we more? For God's sake, I haven't even seen you naked yet!"

"That's what this is about?" Lainey pulled off her shirt and dropped it to the floor.

Cooper's shoulders slumped. "What are you doing?"

"I'm giving you what you want." She reached behind her, undid her bra, dropped it to the floor. Her body was vibrating with anger by the time she'd wrestled the button of her jeans open and pushed the dark denim down. "You want me naked? I'm getting naked."

She stepped out of her jeans, not even caring that she was in the middle of the least sexy, most mechanical striptease ever performed. She stumbled as she tried to get her skinny jeans over one ankle, then off the other. Emotions she couldn't name made the blood thunder in her veins, burned the backs of her eyes, made her skin itch. Despite them, she shoved her underwear down to her knees and let gravity take care of the rest. "There you go, Coop. Your wish is my command."

He didn't look triumphant. He looked miserable, one hand clutching his hair, his other hand on his hip. He

looked like a man surveying the rubble of his domain.
And he was, she supposed, as cool air raised goose
bumps on her skin. The heat of her rage had dissipated.
Instead of a woman proving a point, she was now a pet-
ulant child, finished with her temper tantrum, breathing
hard as she waited to see if it had worked.

Cooper pulled his hand from his hair, dragged it down
his face. He shook his head as he stepped toward her.
His voice was rough, but not with anger, as he pulled
her close and wrapped his arms around her. The sudden
shock of body heat against her flesh made her shiver. She
didn't mean to snuggle against the warm softness of his
T-shirt, but he felt so good right then, strong and solid.

"Christ, Lainey. When you pull shit like this, it makes
me hate how much I like you."

Her voice was small with shame and hope. "You like
me?"

"What the hell did you think this was all about?"

"I guess I just…you said you didn't want to…that you
didn't want me. So I assumed…" Lainey swallowed. His
rejection had been a slap shot in the gut. She wasn't about
to increase the agony by admitting how much it hurt.

"That I didn't want you? Of course I want you! But
not like this." He pulled back a bit, and she tipped her
head back to meet his eyes. "I'm not trying to ruin this
thing. And I'm not asking you to put a name on it. I just
think that, in addition to sex, it might be nice to have
someone to talk to sometimes. Portland is…"

He trailed off, but she could think of a million ways
to fill in the blank: scary, isolated, lonely.

Lainey didn't know what to say. A minute ago, she'd
been desperate for the distraction of sex. But this…
standing naked in his arms as they discussed their fu-

ture, it felt an awful lot like intimacy—and letting people in had never gone well for her. She dropped her gaze. Spoke into his chest, because that felt much safer than making eye contact. "You want us to be friends as well as fuck buddies?"

His chuckle was low, and his arms tightened around her. "Yeah. I guess that's what I'm saying."

"It would be nice to not eat dinner alone at the bar sometimes."

"Then it's settled. We're having dinner tomorrow night. There's a great Vietnamese place two blocks from here. And they deliver. But for now, I think we need to get you into bed. You need some sleep."

She didn't argue, because she was suddenly very tired. It had been a long day.

He swept her into his arms, and after a moment of alcohol-induced vertigo, his apartment righted itself and Lainey decided being held against his chest wasn't the worst place to be. Actually, it made her feel a little better, and considering she was physically naked and emotionally decimated, she supposed that was really something.

Cooper gave her one of his T-shirts to sleep in and she crawled into his giant bed. The white sheets were soft against her skin, and she burrowed into them as he tucked her in.

"Get some sleep. I'm going to go get ready for bed."

"Okay." The word came out as a yawn and her eyes drifted shut.

Lainey thought she felt Cooper press a kiss to her forehead, but she wasn't sure if it had actually happened or if she'd dreamed it.

12

WHEN COOPER WOKE up the next morning, his hand cradling Lainey's breast and his erection pressed against the sweet curve of her ass, he spared a moment to be disgusted by the cliché...until Lainey gave a sleepy sigh and rocked back more snugly against his cock.

He gritted his teeth against the increase in pressure from her innocent movements. He needed to get the hell out of bed and into a cold shower, but when he made a move to disengage, her hand came up to cover his, anchoring it to her breast. Her nipple hardened under his palm, even as she circled her hips against him, leaving no doubt that he'd been mistaken. Her movements were neither sleep-induced, nor innocent.

Cooper breathed a sigh against the back of her neck, giving in to the instinct to rock his own hips, reveling in the hitch of her breath as they indulged in languid, wordless foreplay.

Something had shifted between them last night. She could claim they were nothing but fuck buddies all she wanted. It didn't make it true. She mattered to him. Enough for him to fire his agent. And he mattered to her, too. Why else would she show up at his place, seeking comfort even though she blamed him—or at least his fame—for the pain she was trying to escape?

They'd crossed a relationship threshold that Cooper had never experienced. All he knew was that it felt different, having her in his arms this morning. Sweeter. More real.

His hand drifted down her belly until he reached the hem of the shirt he'd loaned her. It was too big, and hit her midthigh.

Her skin was soft and warm as he traced a line up her leg to her hip, the path unencumbered, since she'd shed her panties in his living room last night before he'd carried her to bed. The heat that had been building slowly through his veins surged with need. He concentrated on the glide of his fingers as he circled her navel, and worked his way back up to squeeze her breast.

With a hum of satisfaction, Lainey shed the T-shirt with as few moves as possible, revealing the delicate width of her back. Entranced, Cooper placed his lips against her shoulder, and wrapped his arm around her waist, pulling her back to him, erasing the space that had been created when she'd disrobed.

Her breath was coming faster now, and their hips moved restlessly, seeking more than was available to them because of his own boxer briefs. Coop grabbed her hip, pushed it forward into the mattress so that Lainey lay on her stomach, her face still turned away from him, her breath coming in shallow pants that mirrored his own.

Cooper shucked his underwear and grabbed a condom from the drawer of the end table. He was desperate for her, but he used every ounce of willpower he had, tamping down the lust, forcing himself to continue the bittersweet torture of discovering her slowly.

Cooper traced the length of her spine with his thumb, watching with hungry fascination as her muscles jumped beneath his touch, enticing him to trace the same path with his lips as he learned every curve, every dip of her.

She shifted on the bed, spreading her legs ever so slightly, and Cooper was helpless to resist the invitation. Lainey moaned as he positioned himself over her, sliding into her from behind. She was so slick, so ready, that she took him in one long, smooth stroke and he pressed against her from chest to thigh, burying his face in the crook of her neck and breathing her in.

LAINEY COULDN'T GET enough of Coop's big body against her back, pinning her to the mattress as he drove inside her, slow and deep. There was something intensely erotic about having his weight on her. It made her feel safe, protected, and in turn she was able to let go of all the bad memories and be in the moment. With him.

Last night, she'd arrived at his door intending to bury her pain and frustration with a quick fuck. Instead, he'd taken care of her. And she'd let him. She'd expected to feel embarrassed this morning, but she'd woken in Cooper's arms with a sense of peace and connection she hadn't known possible.

She'd never doubted their physical connection—that had been apparent from the moment he'd sauntered into her life. But this morning, it was like he could read her mind, too.

He knew just where to touch, when to push harder, when to pull back.

She squeezed her thighs together, loving the increased

friction as he quickened his pace, but more than that, loving the groan that let her know she was reading his mind, too.

Her hand drifted up beside the pillow, and Cooper traced its path, up her forearm, across her injured wrist, until his palm rested against the back of her hand, and their fingers twined together.

Her climax hit like a wave, washing through her with such all-consuming force that she wasn't sure she would survive it.

Cooper rolled onto his back, panting as he stared up at the ceiling. Lainey did the same.

"Holy shit," he said simply.

Lainey glanced over at him, their eyes meeting for the first time that morning. "Wanna go again?"

"Damn straight."

"Coop!"

Bang, bang, bang.

"Coop? C'mon, man. Open the door! I thought we were going for breakfast."

Lainey snapped out of her drowsy euphoria and into alert panic. "Shit! Stop. What are you doing?"

In their quest for sustenance, they'd only made it as far as the couch before getting distracted.

Cooper lifted his head from between her legs, his eyes dark with passion. His voice was rough with frustration. "Don't pretend you don't know what I was doing, because you were close."

"Aren't you going to get the door?"

Cooper gave her a look that eloquently said the thought hadn't even crossed his mind. "Lie back and let me do what I do. Because once I get you off, I've got big plans for the strawberry jam, and the shower, in that order. Stop killing the mood."

Lainey grabbed his hair, but for the first time, it was to keep him from returning to the Promised Land instead of keeping him from leaving. "Listen, Slick. Mood's already DOA. It's been bludgeoned to death. That's my brother at the door! I can't do this when I know he's out there."

Bang, bang, bang.

"Are you seriously gonna leave me out here? I did what you said. No internet at all."

Cooper cut an annoyed gaze at the door as Lainey scrambled to tug her panties up. "*This* is why I don't put people on the list." He rocked back onto his feet and stood up in one fluid movement that held all the predatory grace of a prey cat about to take down a whiny zebra with the shittiest timing ever.

Lainey was distracted for about seven seconds by the shift in his muscles as he adjusted the band of his gray sweatpants, which rode low on his hips. All bulging muscles and bulging...other things. Damned if she wasn't a little turned on despite their unexpected visitor.

"At least put on a shirt!" she hissed, balling up the white tee she'd all but ripped off his body earlier and throwing it at him. It hit him in the shoulder, but he made no move to catch it, letting it drop harmlessly to the hardwood floor.

Lainey scowled at him as she pulled the giant T-shirt he'd loaned her back down her thighs. Cooper looked supremely unconcerned as he made his way to the door and pulled it open. "What?"

"Hey, man." Lainey heard Brett's shoes squeak against the tiles in the foyer as he stepped inside. "I'm starving.

I thought we could watch some game tape and maybe talk about defensive strategy."

"Listen, Brett, now's not really the best time…"

"Fine, I'll pay for breakfast, dude. But only if you're willing to help me out." Brett barged in, too focused on hockey to pick up on all the blatant cues that screamed Cooper was *entertaining*. "Now that we're playing San Jose, I'm worried about getting matched against Gauthier. He's so fast. And it helped, that stuff you said when Cubs kept blowing by me in practice and you told me to support the team and stuff, so I thought… Lainey?"

Damn. This was not how this was supposed to go. Lainey got to her feet, but her words deserted her.

"It's not what you…we never meant to—just let me explain…shit."

Brett's expression went from slack-jawed confusion to deep hurt as he stared at her, then back at Cooper, taking in their respective states of undress, the T-shirt on the floor.

When his gaze cut back to hers, the hurt had given way to anger. Brett's chest was heaving with pent-up rage—he was practically vibrating with it—and Lainey didn't like the way it made her own chest hurt. He turned back to Cooper and his voice cracked with emotion.

"You son of a bitch! First you take my spot on the team, and now you're sneaking around with my sister?" He shoved Cooper hard, but his smaller stature barely had an impact on his muscled opponent.

Cooper's voice was low. Icy. "Sillinger, don't touch me again if you know what's good for you."

Brett's lip trembled, and he looked very young and vulnerable in that moment.

"Brett." Lainey reached out and set a tentative hand

on his shoulder. He whirled around with such speed that she stepped back with surprise.

"What?" The volume of his voice made her wince. "What now? Brett, don't be stupid? Brett, stop bothering us? And to think I thought…" He trailed off with a bitter laugh. "I guess I thought things were different with us now."

"They are different!"

"Whatever, Lainey. Nothing's different. Nothing will ever be different."

He shot a glare at Cooper as he stormed out. "I thought we were friends, man." The slam of the door punctuated Brett's departure.

"We have to go after him!"

Lainey made a move for the door, but Cooper's hand on her shoulder stayed her. "He needs to cool down first. I'll talk to him this afternoon at practice."

"But I—"

"But nothing. He's upset, and he needs to deal with that before he'll be ready to talk. Don't you ever need a little time to process?"

Lainey glanced at the closed door, as if she could see her brother through it somehow. "I guess so."

"I know so. Let's have some food, let the situation decompress."

"I'm not hungry anymore." Guilt had a way of stealing her appetite.

"Then screw the strawberry jam." Cooper slung her over his shoulder in a fireman's carry with such ease that it startled a laugh from her, despite her mood. "Straight to the shower it is."

13

THE PARKING LOT at The Drunken Sportsman was empty when Lainey pulled up in her beat-up Taurus the next morning. Exactly as she'd hoped. It was why she'd come at 9:00 a.m., long before any of the staff were due to arrive. Well, that and she hadn't slept well.

Brett wasn't answering any of her phone calls or texts. She considered trying him again, a last-ditch effort, but he'd be heading to the rink for the morning skate soon, like Cooper had. The Storm started the second round of the playoffs tonight. She'd try him again in the afternoon.

With a sigh, Lainey got out of her car. Her family was once again in shambles, but at least the bar sale was imminent. She was going to read though the contract one more time before Jeannie and the man on the other end of this latest "too good to be true" offer, a Mr. Allan Bashir, arrived at ten for a showing. With any luck, this deal would go through.

Male voices a few feet away pulled her out of her thoughts. There were three guys passing in front of the bar, probably midtwenties, talking loudly and smoking as they headed north on the sidewalk. Lainey kept her head down as she reached back into her car to grab her purse and the contract.

"Is that her?"

"Dude, I totally think that's her. That's the girl on the news."

Lainey took a deep breath, told herself not to over-react. She'd been heckled before. The street wasn't deserted. They wouldn't hurt her when the chance of being caught was so great. She'd let them fob their insults and be on their way.

Slowly, she straightened up with her things and shut the car door.

"It's her. It's gotta be."

They changed direction, started walking toward her. Lainey flipped through her keys, trying to find the one for the Sportsman's front door. If she could get inside and lock it behind her, she'd be okay.

"Hey! You're her, aren't you? Hey! We're talking to you! Least you can do is be polite enough to answer."

Behind her, there was the sound of a car engine, a screech of brakes, and the slamming of a door, but Lainey was too busy trying to get into the bar to pay it much mind. Her hecklers were coming closer, and Lainey couldn't stop her hands from shaking. The key ring slipped from her numb fingers and crashed to the pavement.

"You're the one who scored on your own net and lost us a gold medal!"

"Hey, back off and leave my sister alone!"

Distracted, the leader, a tubby guy in a plaid flannel shirt, adjusted his course to face her rescuer.

A shaky breath escaped her. Brett. Relief left her feeling woozy, and Lainey leaned back against the glass door. She was okay. She and Brett could handle this. Together. The thought gave her strength, and she pulled her phone from her purse as she bent down to grab her keys as Brett approached.

"This national disgrace is your sister?"

"Dude. That's Brett Sillinger. He plays for the Storm." The warning came from the tall skinny henchman.

"I don't care who he is. What I care about is that this bitch cost us a medal."

"Oh, she cost *you* a medal, did she?"

"Brett, forget it." Lainey put a hand on his arm. "It doesn't matter. Let's go inside."

"No way. It does matter." Brett pulled away from her, puffing up his chest as he stepped toward the heckler. It was an odd moment to notice that Brett wasn't a kid anymore. When he'd faced off against Cooper the day before, he'd seemed small to her, but now she could see him as he was. As a man. He'd gotten tall. His chest and shoulders had filled out. Even his playoff beard seemed intimidating rather than scraggly in this moment. There was a reason the guy with the beer paunch took a step back.

"I want to hear all about this douchebag's athletic experience. About what he's so good at that he can represent this country on an international level."

The tubby one didn't back down. "For all the good it did us."

"You're just jealous because even her failures are good enough to be televised. Yours are confined to your mother's basement."

"You punk-ass loser, I—"

"I'm a loser? You're walking around with your buddies yelling insults at women in parking lots!"

"C'mon, Lenny. Let's get out of here, okay?" The third

guy, the quiet one with the ponytail, reached out tugged on his friend's plaid sleeve.

"I hope you choke in the finals," Lenny taunted.

Brett didn't back down. "If I do, I'll still have accomplished more than you ever will."

Without warning, the mouthy one took a swing, clocking Brett in the face before turning and running like a coward. "Let's go!"

The three of them took off down the street, and Lainey placed a hand on Brett's shoulder.

"Oh, my God, Brett. Are you okay?"

He spat some bloody saliva onto the pavement before he straightened up. "I'll live."

"Your lip's a mess." Lainey pulled open the door she'd unlocked earlier. "Come on. Let's get you patched up."

"I thought I wasn't allowed in your bar."

"We're closed. And I don't want your lip to swell up, so we're making an exception."

Lainey made a point of locking the door behind them before she walked Brett over to the bar and pulled out a stool. "Sit. I'll get you some ice."

She dumped her purse and papers on the counter and handed him some paper towel. "Here. Don't bleed on my floor," she warned, before rummaging around for a bag she could fill with ice. Lainey wrapped the makeshift icepack in a towel and turned back to her patient to find Brett dabbing gingerly at his lip.

"Did you know I've never been in a fight before? Not even on the ice. And now I've been in two, and they've both been because of you. At least Coop didn't punch me in the face," he mumbled, wincing as she pressed the bag of ice to his face.

Lainey pulled out the stool beside him and sat down.

"Don't you guys start your series against San Jose tonight? You should be at the arena. What are you doing here?"

"Yeah. I was heading to the rink for the morning skate, but I thought I'd swing by and see if you were here. I wanted to talk to you about yesterday."

"I'm glad you did," she confessed. Now that the adrenaline was dissipating, Lainey realized how differently the situation could have gone. "And I appreciate you standing up for me. A lot of people wouldn't have. You didn't have to."

"Yes, I did! I owe you."

Lainey shook her head. "You don't owe me anything."

"Sure I do. You remember that summer you stayed with us?"

Of course she did. It was the summer her mother had died. The worst summer of her life. And she'd been stuck living with her dad and his new family.

"And I was begging you to come play street hockey with me, but you wouldn't."

A twinge of guilt tightened her chest. She'd been a bitch that summer, and Brett had been nothing more to her than her dad's devil spawn, the nuisance she couldn't shake.

"So I was out hitting the ball against the garage door, and the Peroni boys from a few doors down had a game going with some of the neighborhood kids, but they'd never let me play because I was too young. And they started heckling me, calling me a baby and saying I shot like a girl."

The memory flirted at the edge of her brain, becoming clearer with every detail Brett added. She'd blocked most of that summer from her mind, remembering it only as a long, dark tunnel she'd had to endure without her mother, the only person who'd loved her. But she could see it now, a street full of twelve- and thirteen-year-old boys.

"You grabbed my stick, marched out to the middle of the road and drilled a shot past Jian, who was the best goaltender in the neighborhood, and then you said—"

"'How's that for shooting like a girl?'" Lainey smiled as she and Brett said the words together.

"And you followed it up by telling them if they ever hoped to touch a girl's boobs, they'd better stop acting like misogynistic assholes."

Lainey did not remember that part. "I said that?"

"Yeah. After you walked away, the game broke up so they could all run home and look up what misogynistic meant." Brett flinched when he smiled, pressing the bag against his split lip. "But they let me play after that."

"Really?"

"Yeah. I mean, your talk of touching girls' boobs jump-started puberty in the neighborhood, so I had to steal them one of your bras first, but they let me play."

"You perv!" Lainey shoved Brett, but her laughter gave her away. "I wondered where that purple bra went!"

Brett's chuckle dissolved in a wince. "Ow. Don't make me laugh." He readjusted the ice pack.

They sat in silence for a long moment.

"I think that trying to keep up with those guys is what made me a better hockey player. So that's kind of because of you. And you were doing so great, with your hockey scholarship and stuff. I wanted to be just like you. That was kind of my last good summer."

Lainey frowned at the sentiment. "What?"

Brett sighed. "I was excited that you were there. My mom would tell me to leave you alone, because of what happened with your mom and all. She said you were sad, and you needed space. I wanted to hang out with you. I wanted to be good at hockey like you were. And I didn't want to be an only child. But you left for college at the end of the summer.

"It was all downhill after that. Mom and Dad got divorced that winter. I dunno. It was probably good. It's the reason that I tried so hard. I guess I wanted to impress you. I know you picked number 42 because Dad wore it, but I picked it because of you."

The quiet confession detonated like a bomb, and Lainey couldn't find words through the emotional shrapnel.

"I thought for sure you'd call when I made the league."

"I should have. But truthfully? I was jealous."

"You were?"

Lainey nodded. "I thought you had everything. You had Dad. Your mom was still alive. You were a hockey superstar and my career was in tatters. I resented you. You were this annoying little kid with everything I ever wanted in life. I was petty, and I'm sorry."

"Yeah, well. You didn't miss much. Dad was always either sleeping off a hangover or here." Brett looked around the dingy bar. "And Mom, well, she's been husband hunting ever since they split up. In fact, I called her to let her know we made the playoffs, but she's in Cabo right now, about to hook husband number four, so she can't get away this month."

Brett shook his head, and it was the first time Lainey had ever seen him look jaded. "Sorry you wasted all that jealousy, because the grass was the exact same shade of brown on my side of the fence."

Lainey was ashamed she hadn't realized it before. "It

wasn't all wasted. You really are a good hockey player, Brett. But it's not because of me. You did that on your own. And I'm impressed."

"I wish the guys were impressed. But they think of me as a kid. It's my second year in the league and they still call me rookie. No one ever wants to hang out. And then Cooper started helping me with my game. And I thought maybe, if we hung out a bit... I dunno. It was stupid."

Brett shrugged, dropped his gaze. "He said things were fine between us at practice yesterday, but I think he was just being nice because you and I are related. And now you guys are...uh, you know. And I mean, what happens if you break up? Coop already doesn't like me that much... It's gonna be worse if I'm his ex's brother. And what about you? You're never gonna come watch me play because he'll be there."

Every word Brett spoke stung like a dart in Lainey's chest. "I'm going to give you some unsolicited advice right now. Stop trying so hard."

"What?" He lowered the bag and frowned at her.

"Brett, just be you. You're actually kind of a cool guy when you're not trying to make people like you."

The stunned expression on his face was priceless. "You think I'm cool?"

She laughed. "I do, actually. Especially after today. Thank you for sticking up for me."

His look was matter-of-fact. "You're my sister."

For the first time, those words made her feel warm, like maybe the only reason she'd spent so long feeling as if she didn't belong anywhere was because she was too scared to let herself.

"Yeah." Lainey slugged Brett in the shoulder. "Yeah, I am."

They sat for a moment, letting that sink in.

"You know, a normal sister would have gone for a hug just then."

"Let's not push it."

14

"THIS IS HOLLY EVANS, reporting live from the Storm's locker room in the Portland Dome, and with me is defenseman Cooper Mead. Cooper, your team has had a dominant performance so far in the playoffs, having already swept the Wyoming Stallions. With tonight's shutout win, you've put San Jose on notice. How does it feel to know that your team is coming together at the right time?"

Cooper wiped the sweat from his face with the Women's Sport Network towel Holly had slung over his shoulder before the camera started rolling. "It feels great. We're definitely ready. We played hard tonight, and we got results. I'm especially proud of how the younger guys are stepping up. We all have something to prove this year, and it's been great to see that drive translating into dominant performances on the ice."

"So you think you guys have a shot at going all the way?"

"Definitely. Like you said, we've really gelled over the last month and a half. Our defense, in particular, has been working hard to support Mack. He put on a hell of show between the pipes during our first series, but you're not going to win a championship if your goaltender has to do all the work."

"Last question before I let you go, the thing that's on everyone's mind…"

He braced himself for a question about Lainey.

"Cooper, tell me, what's it like to be a meme?"

She'd softballed him, and he tried not to let his gratitude show.

"It's been quite an experience. The guys give me a hard time about it." He shot a winning smile at the camera. "But it's better than having no one know your name."

"Care to tell us the story behind that photo?"

"I think this might be one of those moments when the mystery is more interesting than the story. Besides, I like seeing the captions people are coming up with."

"Well, there you have it, Cooper Mead, Man of Mystery. Thanks for taking time out of your busy schedule. As a sports journalist, I'm impartial, but off the record, I happen to have a vested interest in cheering the Storm on to victory."

Cooper grinned at the reference to her relationship with Luke. "Well, it'll be our little secret then, even though I know a certain team captain who will be glad to hear it."

They shared a chuckle for the camera, and Holly wished him luck. Then her camera guy signaled they were clear.

"Jay, I'd like to grab a comment from Eric before we wrap." Holly handed the mic to him.

"Sure thing, Hols. I'll go set up."

With her business taken care of, she turned back to Cooper, holding her ground amid the rest of the reporters jostling to shove their own microphones in his face. "Listen, Cooper, I'd love to have you on my show for a full hour sometime when you're not in the middle of the playoff grind, if you're interested. I think my listeners would love to ask you some questions of their own."

"Yeah, sure. That would be great." The Women's Sport Network was one of XT Satellite Radio's biggest draws, and that didn't even include the numbers her website brought in. In fact, his agent—*ex-agent*, Cooper reminded himself—had tried to get him on a few times when he still played for New York.

"Speaking of being on the show…" Holly trailed off, but her tone had Cooper bracing to return the favor he owed her for letting him off easy in the interview. Although he couldn't imagine who the hell on the team he had more sway over than her boyfriend did. Maguire was the captain for a reason. The guys respected the hell out of him.

"Luke mentioned that you and Elaine Sillinger…know each other."

That was one way to put it.

"We've met," Coop confirmed drily.

"I know she's a little shy when it comes to reporters."

"If 'shy' is code for hating all media with the passion of a thousand rabid badgers, then yeah. She's a little shy."

"Look, I know she got her ass handed to her after Vancouver, but now that the cat is out of the bag, the hounding isn't going to stop. Can you let her know if she ever wants to make a comment on the record, she only needs to call?"

Holly handed him her business card, and Cooper took it, even though he wasn't sure Lainey would be interested.

"No bullshit, no sneak attack, just a chance to clear the air."

"I'll let her know. But I wouldn't cut the promo reel yet. And if you want a chance in hell at scoring this interview, then you'd better not call her Elaine to her face. She prefers Lainey."

Holly smiled. "I appreciate the tip."

Cooper answered a few more questions before it was time for the reporters to leave the dressing room. Not that his night was over. After the team hit the showers and were looking respectable in their suits, they'd file out for the more formal interviews and the postgame press conference. It would be another couple of hours before he got home, but he couldn't wait that long to talk to Lainey. After he'd tugged off his jersey, shoulder pads and elbow pads, he grabbed his phone and headed to a quieter corner of the dressing room to call her.

"Hello?"

"Hey, we won."

"That's amazing. Congratulations, Coop."

"Thanks. Actually, I wanted to tell you that I got some good news before the game. You know the kid from the Children's Hospital I was telling you about? Danny? His doctors have cleared him to come to a game as long as he has some equipment and a nurse on hand, so the team has agreed to give him and his family one of the luxury boxes. I get to tell him tomorrow, and I was wondering if you would come with me?"

There was an awkward silence. Cooper knew the idea of being seen in public, especially with him, was not high on Lainey's list of priorities right now.

"I'd like you to meet him," he added, hoping to sway her in the right direction.

She was quiet for another few seconds before she relented. "Yeah, okay. I'll go."

"That's great. Thank you. I'll pick you up tomorrow around noon."

"I'll be ready."

"Oh, hey. Before you hang up—do you know what happened to Brett's face? He's strutting around here being all mysterious and low-key with his busted lip. And he had his best game of the season. It's not like him at all."

Another silence, but this one held no awkwardness. In fact, Coop was pretty sure Lainey was smiling when she finally spoke.

"No idea. Maybe he's growing up. I'll see you tomorrow, Slick."

THE WOMAN WHO met them outside Danny's room looked both thrilled and exhausted to the core. Lainey's heart went out to her. Having a sick child was a strain she couldn't even imagine.

"Danny. You've got a special visitor."

"Coop! What are you doing here?" The boy's excitement was adorable, and when Lainey glanced over, Cooper's smile was almost as big.

"Lainey," he said, as the two of them approached the kid's bed, "this is my buddy, Danny. Danny, this is—" There was a weird pause as Cooper grappled for how to introduce her, but the owl-eyed youngster saved them both.

"Elaine Sillinger. Number 42. Nickname: The Ice Queen. Defenseman. You scored on your own net and cost your team the gold."

Coop swallowed a laugh, and Lainey shot him a quick

frown before she stuck her hand out to shake Danny's. "Charmed, I'm sure."

The kid accepted the handshake without missing a beat. "What a lot of people don't know is that you were also the top-scoring defenseman for three years running in the NCAA."

Lainey's gaze turned assessing. "Huh. Maybe you're not so bad after all."

"I grow on people," Danny announced without a hint of guile.

"Like a fungus," Cooper teased. "Well, Lainey and I are here with some good news. Looks like you and your family are going to be my special guests at one of our playoff games!"

It took a moment for the news to sink in. "You mean I get to go? To the Portland Dome?" Danny looked at his mom for confirmation, waiting for her to nod before he let the smile work its way across his freckled face.

It didn't quite make it to fruition before he looked far too serious for a ten-year-old again. "Is this because I'm sick?"

"It's because we're friends," Cooper countered.

The kid didn't bite. "Yeah, but we're only friends because I'm sick."

"Then yeah, I guess it's because you're sick." Cooper's tone was matter-of-fact.

Danny nodded, and Lainey got the impression that the kid appreciated being told the truth. "All right, I'll go."

They stayed for another ten minutes, talking hockey while Danny's mom took photos to commemorate the occasion.

"Hey, Coop? Before you go, can I ask you something?"

"Sure. Anything."

"How come you haven't asked me why I'm in here?"

Cooper sat back down. "Because it doesn't matter why you're here to me. And I figured you'd tell me if you wanted me to know."

Danny sat quietly for a moment, absorbing that. "Can we still be like normal even if I tell you?"

"Definitely."

"I have *os-te-o-sar-coma*." Danny said each syllable slowly and with extreme precision. "That's a fancy world for bone cancer. If chemotherapy doesn't work, they might have to amputate my leg."

Lainey's heart sank, and she could see the sadness in Cooper's eyes. "That's rough. Scary, I bet."

Danny shrugged. "I used to play hockey when I was little, you know. Before. But if they cut off my leg then I'm not going to be able to do anything."

"That's not true!" Coop wrestled his emotions back under control. Lowered his voice. "You know who Luke Maguire's brother is?"

Danny didn't disappoint him. "Ethan Maguire, Number 10. Centerman. Nickname: Flash. Gold medalist. Played for the Wisconsin Blades. Hockey career was cut short when he got hit from behind."

Cooper leaned forward, bracing his elbows on his knees. "Then you know he's in a wheelchair now."

"Yeah."

"And you also know he's on the playoff hockey panel for *Portland News Now* and he writes a bunch of stuff for *Sports Nation*. And I'll bet he doesn't know half the stats you know. So you'll probably be able to take his job in a few years. Because you don't have to play hockey to be part of hockey."

"I guess."

"Or get some other amazing job. You're really smart."

"Nobody cares about that. People make fun of me for reading all the time."

"Those guys are jealous."

Danny looked skeptical. "I don't think so."

"I do. Because I know I'm jealous of it." Something about the way he said it caught Lainey's attention. It wasn't patronizing. It wasn't flattery. It rang of truth.

Danny face was the picture of confusion. "Huh? No, you aren't."

Cooper glanced up at her, and she could see the indecision in his eyes. The weight of his stare was palpable, almost like he was asking her for something. She sat back down in the chair beside him.

His next breath was so deep it seemed to strain the material of his T-shirt.

"Kid, I'm gonna tell you a secret. And you can't tell anyone."

Danny's eyes widened at the prospect. "I won't. Cross my heart." He did, to prove he meant it.

Cooper stared at the kid for a moment, but when he finally spoke, he looked right at her. "I have dyslexia."

His words stunned her. Snippets of their time together played through her memory like a flipbook: how he asked the server for suggestions at the restaurant, how he called instead of texting, how he always asked what she was reading instead of looking at the titles himself.

All endearing gestures on their own, but now she could see they went deeper than the veil of charm she'd always attributed them to. They were tactics that had been carefully honed over a lifetime of secret keeping. Survival skills. She recognized them well.

She reached out and squeezed his knee, leaving her

hand there as his shoulders relaxed and he turned back to Danny.

"You know what that is?"

Danny shook his head.

"It means I have trouble reading."

"You can't read?"

Cooper smiled wryly. "Not exactly. It's more that my brain gets the letters jumbled up, so it's tricky for me to figure out words. I have to concentrate really hard to make words make sense."

"Like a puzzle. You know when you dump it out of the box, and you know it's gonna be a picture, but it isn't one yet."

"Yeah. Like that. And that's why I didn't want to read you that magazine the first time I was here. And I didn't want to tell you…" Again, Cooper met her eyes and she knew his words were for her as much as for Danny. "Because I used to get made fun of pretty bad when I was your age. People called me stupid, knocked me around. And it made me believe that I was dumb. That I wasn't as good as them."

Danny considered that for a moment. "Yeah, I feel that way sometimes, when people make fun of me for reading instead of playing with them. They don't understand I'm too tired."

"It's hard not to care what other people think of you sometimes," Cooper told him, and Lainey's heart broke a little.

"But I still like you, even if you can't read. Hey, maybe during my chemo, you could come by, and I could read to you!"

There was a stinging sensation behind the bridge of

Lainey's nose, and her eyes watered as Cooper patted Danny's bony little shoulder. "I'd like that, kid."

They said their goodbyes, and Cooper and Lainey walked through the hallway toward the bank of elevators.

When they stepped inside, Lainey hit the button for the lobby. "Why didn't you tell me before?"

He shook his head, as if he was at a loss. "My parents are both professors—Dad's an English literature buff and Mom's a linguist. How's that for irony? And I know they love me, but I also know that neither of them were hoping their only child would be a dumb jock. They're good people, and I can't imagine my life without them, but we don't have a lot in common, you know?"

The confession cost him. She could see it in the way he kept his gaze on the floor, took up less space than he usually did. "You already made your views on hockey players clear. I guess I didn't want you to think I was stupid on top of it."

Lainey grabbed his hand, squeezed it. "You're not a dumb jock. You're a world-class defenseman who has dyslexia, and you don't ever have to feel embarrassed with me."

It wasn't until they passed the third floor that he finally squeezed her back.

THIRTY MINUTES LATER, they were at the Vietnamese place Cooper loved, sitting at a table in the back corner, waiting for their takeout.

The hospital visit had kicked his ass, emotionally speaking, and the fact that Lainey hadn't laughed at him—or worse, pitied him—meant more than she would ever know. And since he'd already broached one terrifying subject with her today, he figured he might as well cross the other one off the list, too.

"So, I have something for you."

Lainey sat straighter in the rickety chair, intrigued.

"Don't get too excited." Cooper dug through his wallet. "I don't think you're going to like it much."

She took the business card he held out and he could see by her suspicious look that she recognized Holly Evans's name. "Why are you giving me this?"

"She wants to interview you."

Lainey shook her head. "I don't want to talk about that."

"I know you don't, but trust me, as a guy who's weathered a couple of not-so-great media moments, it might help to get out in front of this. Deal with it and move on."

"I scored on my own net." The words came out small and meek.

"Lainey, that's part of the game. You screwed up. We've all done it. So sure, every four years, that video will make the rounds again, and it's embarrassing and it sucks. But that's life with the internet.

"Google 'Cooper Mead fuckups' sometime. There's an eight-minute compilation video on YouTube of me tripping over the blue line, winding up for a slap shot and not making contact with the puck—even the time I shattered the rink glass when I went flying into the boards and completely missed the guy I was trying to body check."

A flicker of a smile wobbled on her lips. "I actually remember that."

"Me, too. I remember every single one of those moments, but there's no way that I'm going to miss a game because of them."

"So the moral of the story is that you love hockey?"

"More than anything in the world."

She shrugged. "That's great for you, but I don't see how it applies to me."

Her voice sounded unaffected, but Cooper noticed how she cradled her scarred wrist.

She followed the direction of his gaze immediately and frowned. "I didn't give up, if that's what you're thinking. After the goal that shook America, I went back to my college team. First period of my first game back, there's a scrum in the corner, I get tripped up and I hit the ice. That scar you're staring at?" She held out her wrist. "Three hours in surgery, and the end of my career. I didn't just give hockey up. I tried to fight for it."

Cooper wasn't trying to pick a fight. "Look, this decision is completely up to you. But I know how draining it is to hide something about yourself. It eats at you."

Cooper shrugged. "You keep punishing yourself for a mistake that could've happened to anyone. Your teammate has forgiven you. You have to find a way to forgive yourself, because you're the only one standing in your way now. This interview with Holly might be a good first step."

Their conversation was interrupted as the pretty Vietnamese girl who'd taken their order brought two bags of food to their table. "Here you go. Grandma threw in a couple of free egg rolls because she thinks you're handsome."

Cooper laughed as he got to his feet. "Thank her for me, Linh."

She frowned at him. "No way. That'll only encourage her. Enjoy the food, you two."

Lainey waited until Linh was back behind the counter before she heaved a deep sigh and stood up. "Okay."

Cooper grinned. "Okay, you'll do the interview?" he asked, grabbing a bag in each hand.

"Okay, I'll think about it," she countered. "Now stop with that stupid, handsome smile that gets you free food and makes people think about things they don't want to do."

He did his best to comply.

15

TWO WEEKS LATER, Lainey found herself standing on a picturesque Portland street, realizing how much had changed since she'd agreed to this meeting with sports reporter Holly Evans. For one, Cooper and the Storm had blown past San Jose and were now in the midst of a hard-fought third-round battle with the Montana Wolfpack. Secondly, this street, which she'd wandered often in her youth, had changed so much as to be almost unrecognizable to her. And last but not least, her mind, because Lainey was 99 percent sure this meeting was going to be a colossal waste of time.

All of Coop's rah-rah talk about facing fears and kicking ass were fine in theory. But now that the moment was upon her, the urge to curl up and let the media storm recede, at least until the next batch of "biggest hockey screwups" YouTube videos resurrected the footage again, seemed like the smart plan.

No. She was going to meet with Holly, Lainey decided. Because she never again wanted to feel the way she had when Lenny and his henchmen had cornered her outside the bar. And because if a ten-year-old boy could face bone cancer with enough grace and dignity to make Cooper Mead cry, then she had no right to be cowardly over this.

Lainey looked up at the teal-and-white-striped awning with the word "Icing" printed on it in a simple, serif font. She glanced at her phone to make sure she was in the right place. She'd been expecting a different bakery, called Piece of Cake, but the address matched, and Lainey found herself a little sad to realize it must have closed since her last visit all those years ago.

When she was young, she'd been allowed to pick out one of the beautiful, six-layer cakes that beckoned from the display case on her birthday. The owner, Stella, had been this lovely, grandmotherly figure who'd always made Lainey feel grown-up, like *she* was the customer instead of her mother.

And during her very difficult return to Portland after her mother had died, she'd spent a lot of time at the bakery, choosing to do her homework there with the happy memories of her mom, rather than at her father's house, where she felt like a stranger.

She was surprised at the rush of emotion as she stepped through the door.

"Lainey!" At the sound of her name, she walked toward the woman in the far corner of the bakery.

"Thank you so much for coming. I'm Holly."

The gorgeous blonde stood and extended her hand for Lainey to shake.

"Well, thank you for meeting me here. I appreciate it."

Lainey glanced around the cupcake store. Matte-gray rectangular floor tiles, sleek white booths that featured both vibrant flowers in teal mason jars and iPads for at-table ordering. Rows upon rows of tempting cupcakes in a rainbow of appetizing pastels and handwritten chalk-boards detailing their menu. It was a surprising mix of homespun and state-of-the-art, and while Lainey missed the old-fashioned predecessor for sentimental reasons, she found she liked Icing's atmosphere. And the fact that it smelled like she'd died and gone to olfactory heaven didn't hurt. "You do all your preinterview vetting while on a sugar high?"

"Whenever I can."

Lainey liked her matter-of-factness. "I respect that."

"For the record, I think this is a brave way to handle your recent media storm."

"For the record, I'm still strongly considering going with 'no comment,' so don't be too impressed yet."

Holly's chuckle seemed genuine. "I can see why Cooper likes you. Please, have a seat."

The invitation stole the smile from Lainey's lips, even as she slid into the booth. Luckily a pretty brunette approached the table and saved her from having to reply. She had no idea where Holly had gotten the idea that Cooper liked her. Okay, he liked her, sure, but he didn't *like* like her. At least not in the way that made complete strangers comment on it.

"Hi, I'm Rebecca. You must be Lainey."

"Oh. Yeah. Hey." Lainey couldn't remember the last time she'd shaken so many hands.

"Welcome to Icing."

"Thanks. I thought… I mean, you wouldn't happen to know anything about the woman who ran the bakery that used to be here, would you?"

"You know Stella?" Rebecca's smile was beaming, and the tightness around Lainey's heart loosened. Surely her reaction would have been more subdued if anything untoward had happened to Stella.

"Yeah, I mean, sort of. My mom and I used to come here." Lainey kept her answers noncommittal.

Rebecca had no such compunctions, and dove head-first into an update. "Stella's fantastic! She and her beau moved to Paris. They got married on New Year's Eve in the little patisserie where she works a few mornings a week. It was adorable. I've never seen her look so happy. Eric, on the other hand, was a total wreck when he gave her away." Rebecca shook her head fondly. "That man worries more than anyone I've ever met. This playoff run might be the death of him."

"Eric Jacobs?" Lainey asked. She'd never met him, since she was a couple of years older than he was, but Stella had spoken often of her grandson during Lainey's trips to the bakery, and his name had been bandied about in hockey circles, even back then.

"They're dating, if you can't tell by the dreamy smile on her face," Holly teased.

Blushing, Rebecca pressed her hands to her cheeks. "Sorry, you guys! You're here to do business and I'm rambling on. Did you know what you want, Lainey? Because no matter how hard I try, I can't get Holly to get anything besides the vanilla bean cupcake and Earl Grey tea."

"I don't suppose you sell Stella's pink lemonade cake in cupcake form?"

"Of course we do! And it goes perfectly with our strawberry green tea. You ladies talk business and I'll be back with your desserts."

"So, Lainey, I don't want to waste anyone's time here.

What's it going to take to get you to say yes to this interview?"

Cupcakes and straight talk. Lainey found she liked Holly Evans very much.

"I guess I want to know why you think I should. I mean, it's an old story that's been done to death. Sure, it's flared up a little because of my…affiliation with Cooper Mead, but there's nothing new to report."

"I disagree completely," Holly told her, pausing for a moment as Rebecca placed their tea and cupcakes in front of them before disappearing back into the kitchen. "I think you've shied away from the media since it happened, and so they are the ones who've controlled the narrative. I'm offering you the chance to tell your side of the story."

Lainey picked the glossy strawberry off the top of her cupcake and popped it into her mouth, chewing thoughtfully. After all this time hiding, could it be that putting it all out there was the answer to getting her life back in order?

Cooper's words rang in her ears. *You're the only one standing in your way now.*

Maybe he was right. But now Fate was giving her the perfect chance to clear the air and put the entire fiasco behind her. She'd be a fool not to take it.

Decision made, Lainey reached for her cupcake. "You know what? You talk a good game, Holly Evans. I'm in."

LAINEY HAD JOINED Holly in her studio three days later, and the Women's Sport Network interview had been a smashing success. The callers had been incredibly supportive, and while internet trolls and haters like Lenny and his crew still existed, they seemed less daunting to her now that she knew there were people who were on her side, people who'd failed and moved on, like she was trying to do. Hockey was her past, and it didn't have to control her anymore. In fact, her present was going pretty darn well.

She and Coop had fallen into a routine. When Cooper was on the road, he'd FaceTime her from whatever fancy hotel room he was staying in. When the games were in town, she'd head over to his place after her bar shift was over. Cooper had even given her a key and cleared her with Pete and the rest of his doorman cronies. She told herself she spent so much time there because his rain-head shower and Jacuzzi tub were state-of-the art, and much better than her downgraded hotel accommodations, but while that was definitely true, there were other reasons. Reasons that made her palms itch and her chest tighten. Reasons that she wasn't quite ready to name for fear that if she did, she might not be the same person anymore.

She glanced over at Brett, who was still shoving clothes into his suitcase even though he was due at the airport in a little over an hour. She stood impatiently in her brother's apartment, waiting for him to show her the ins and outs of feeding his stupid betta fish while he was on the road because his housekeeping service was out of commission thanks to the flu.

"Hurry up! I need to get to Cooper's to say goodbye before he leaves."

"I'm hurrying. You've got the key already. Just read the back of the food pellets. Brett Jr. is on the dining room table."

Lainey rolled her eyes. He'd named his fish Brett Jr., because of course he had. She wandered in the fish's general direction, but was distracted by the ring of her phone. Her screen lit up with a photo of her Realtor's toothy smile.

"Hi, Jeannie. Tell me the good news. Are you at your office? I can meet you in two hours to sign…What do you mean he rescinded the offer? Is he there right now? Put him on." Lainey tapped her foot as she waited for Allan Bashir to get on the line.

"Hello?"

"Mr. Bashir. It's Lainey Harper. Jeannie said you changed your mind about our deal?"

"It's not a deal until the paperwork is signed. Someone else made me an offer I couldn't refuse."

Lainey shook her head, rejecting the rejection. She needed this sale. "What can I do to change your mind back?"

"Final-round playoff tickets and ten thousand dollars are of more use to me than your bar. I liked the location, but there are others that will do just as well. It's a good piece of property. You will sell soon. But it won't be to be me. Good day, Ms. Harper."

The click seemed to reverberate through her body with the finality of the slam of a door.

Brett emerged from his room with his suitcase. "Okay, I think I'm ready." He flopped into his recliner and pulled out his phone. "Did you have any questions about the fish stuff? Hello? Earth to Lainey."

"It's over. He's not buying the bar. He changed his mind."

"Sucks. Sorry." Brett mumbled the words, thumbs tapping furiously against the screen.

"It does. It really does. We were so close to a deal, and then he changes his mind? Because of hockey tickets?

And who would pay him to not buy the bar? It doesn't make any sense..." Lainey frowned as the pieces started to fit together. Brett was engrossed in his phone, refusing to make eye contact.

When you're on the team, there are ways of getting tickets.

A hollow feeling settled in the pit of her stomach.

"What did you do? Brett, what did you do?"

"He wasn't the right guy! He jammed out of your deal for a couple of playoff games and some cash! How does a guy like that deserve Dad's bar?"

"It's not Dad's bar! He left it to me, Brett. It's *my* bar. And I can do whatever I want with it. I can't believe you sabotaged this deal! Did you do this before?" The realization stunned her. "Is this why all of the other offers fell through? Is this why you were asking Cooper for hockey tickets?"

Brett's lack of denial was as good as a confession. "I thought if you couldn't sell it, you might stay."

"That's not fair, Brett. I have plans for my life, too."

"Why do they have to be in LA? Or wherever the hell else you go? What's wrong with here?"

"I have a job to get back to! I haven't taken an assignment in weeks."

"The bar can be your job."

She shook her head. She didn't know how to explain it to him. She didn't want to live with ghosts, and Portland was full of ghosts for her.

"You're just like him. Family means nothing to you." Brett said the words quietly, but they echoed like a gunshot. She braced herself with a hand on the wall, as the impact made her stagger.

"How dare you say that to me?" The hurtful comparison spurred her into action, and she pulled his keys from her pocket and set them on the arm of the couch. "Find someone else to feed your stupid fish." Lainey headed for the door.

"See? You're bailing right now. Just like you always do. Just like he did."

Brett raised his voice to ensure she heard him as she pulled the door shut behind her.

16

COOPER STARED OUT the floor-to-ceiling window in his master bedroom. This apartment had a hell of a view of the city, he decided as he made the final loop with his black silk tie and shimmied his Windsor knot into place.

Lainey had said she'd stop by after her meeting and say goodbye before the car service came to take him to the airport.

After flying through the first three stages of the play-offs, the Storm had finally met their match, and the Wisconsin Blades were proving to be worthy opponents. In less than an hour, he and his team would be winging their way East, down a game and in danger of elimination. He should be nervous about that. But he wasn't. He was nervous about the tickets in the breast pocket of his suit jacket, which was currently laid out on the foot of the bed.

Tickets he was going to give to Lainey when he asked her if she'd consider coming to watch him play.

When Cooper had taken the trade to Portland, he'd been thinking about nothing but hockey. Get in, win the championship, do what needed to be done. To his surprise, his time with the Storm had been about so much more than that. Seeing how settled his teammates were—the lives guys like Luke and Eric were building—had changed his perspective. The sport was important to them, but they also had people they cared about, causes they were committed to.

And here he was, in his thirties, and the teammate he had the most in common with was a teenager.

He had a few good years of hockey left in him, he knew that, but for the first time, Cooper found himself thinking about his life after that. About who he wanted to share it with. He understood why she'd kept her distance. He'd seen his share of guys shy away from the arena after a career-ending injury. Plus all that stuff with her dad? But if he and Lainey were going to be something...

The muffled bang of the condo's front door stole his attention. "You are not going to believe what happened to me."

Speaking of which...

Cooper exhaled, a futile attempt to calm the flurry of nerves in his stomach, and grabbed his suit jacket, tugging it on as he walked out of the bedroom.

"You remember all that nice stuff I said about Brett finally growing up? I take it back."

Lainey put her purse on the coffee table and walked over to him. "That's a nice suit. You look good in blue," she said, reaching up to straighten his tie before she pressed a kiss to his lips.

It was all so...domestic, her fussing over him, telling him about her day.

Cooper reached out and grabbed her around the waist, pulling her close so he could kiss her long and slow and proper.

"What was that for?" Lainey looked dazed when he finally let her go.

"Just felt like it. What did Brett do now?"

His question shattered the dreamy expression his kiss had inspired and he followed along as she took off for the kitchen with a frown. "You know all those great offers on the bar that keep falling through at the last minute?" She tugged open the fridge to peruse the selection. "That was all him. He's been bribing them so I'd be stuck with the bar!"

Lainey grabbed a bottle of water, offered him one, but Cooper shook his head.

"But you don't actually feel stuck with the bar anymore, do you?" Cooper chose his words carefully. "I mean, it's been going well, right? You're getting along better with the staff. It's turning a profit."

She twisted the cap off her bottle and took a drink. "You sound like him. It's better, sure, but if you're asking me if I want to keep the Sportsman and run it until the end of time, then no. In fact, I'm considering closing it down. It might be easier to unload as a lot. The real estate agent mentioned the option before. I guess if I'm ever going to get out of this place, it's time to explore it."

Coop tugged on his tie. It was strangling him all of a sudden. "Oh. That's great. That you have options."

She cocked a brow at him. "You don't sound like you think it's great."

"No, it's… I'm just…surprised. And a bit distracted by all your news. I wanted to talk to you about something before I left, but now…this might not be the right moment."

Lainey capped her water and set it on the counter beside her. "Go ahead, Slick. I'm rapt with attention."

Well, shit.

What the hell was he supposed to do with this?

"I was, I mean, tomorrow night in Wisconsin is a do-or-die game for us. But if we win…" Coop reached into the breast pocket of his suit, bypassing his phone for the tickets he'd stowed there. "Well, if we win, then we'll be coming back to play in Portland, and these tickets are going to be worth a whole lot."

"Oh, my God, are those game seven tickets?"

Lainey's eyes rounded at the sight, and Cooper relaxed a little.

Tell her how you feel.

"They are." He held them out to her. "And I wanted you to have them, because it would mean a lot if—"

Lainey threw herself into his arms before he finished the sentence. "Are you kidding me?" She laughed, and Coop couldn't have wiped the goofy grin that had overtaken his face if you'd paid him. She pulled back, accepting the tickets and inspecting them. "These are incredible seats! I can get him back!"

"Sorry, what?" His grin withered.

"He killed our deal for playoff tickets and ten grand. If I give him these and drop the price by twelve grand, there's no way Mr. Bashir won't reconsider. You just sold my bar, Slick!"

Cooper stood there. He had a weird feeling in his chest, almost like his heart was buzzing. Was that shock setting in? It took a long moment before he realized the sensation was due to the vibration of his phone. He fumbled it out of his pocket and answered. "Mead. Okay, I'll be right down."

Lainey frowned. "Coop? Are you okay? You're acting weird all of a sudden."

"What? Yeah." He shook his head to clear the fuzzy feeling. "I'm fine. I gotta go. The car service is here."

"Okay. Have a safe flight. And good luck tomorrow night. I know you guys can beat the Blades." She planted a kiss on his cheek. "And thanks again for the tickets."

Cooper vaguely remembered nodding as he walked to the foyer, grabbed his suitcase and headed down to meet his driver.

17

LAINEY WAS IN the mood to celebrate.

At least she had been.

Now that two in the morning had come and gone, sleep was sounding much better than the cupcakes she'd picked up from Icing on her way over to Cooper's place to wait for him to get home. The offer of the playoff tickets had been a success, and her Realtor had set up a meeting with Bashir to finalize the sale of The Drunken Sportsman two days from now, and she couldn't wait to thank Coop properly for all he'd done to help her accomplish it.

The team was taking a red-eye charter flight back from Milwaukee after the game, which they'd won 1-0 according to her quick Google search. She'd been confident in her ability to stay up and greet him when he came through the door. And she still could, she decided, turning down the volume on the television and burrowing into the corner of Cooper's massive leather couch with the comforter she'd pulled off the bed. She just needed a quick nap first, she told herself as her eyes drifted shut.

Lainey started as the door slammed followed by the sound of someone stumbling into the condo.

Adrenaline had her on her feet in the ultimate show of fight or flight, until Cooper's familiar form became visible in the flickering light of the big-screen TV. Heart thundering, Lainey exhaled with relief. "Oh, my God, Slick. You scared me half to death."

"Lainey?"

"You were expecting someone else?"

His smile was a little off-kilter as he came fully into the living room. "You're funny. And really pretty. Have I told you how funny and really pretty you are?"

The compliment seemed sincere, but Lainey frowned all the same. Something was wrong. Cooper was slurring his words, banging around like he was drunk, but there was no way the team had provided booze on the charter plane in the middle of playoffs.

She reached over and flicked on the floor lamp beside the couch, and Cooper winced at the light as she took in his rumpled appearance—his tie askew, his hair sweaty.

"Are you okay, Cooper?"

His emphatic nod threw him off balance and Lainey lunged forward to steady him.

"Maybe you should sit down. That's right." She managed to get him to the couch.

"I'm better than okay," he assured her, but though his voice sounded steadier, the ten seconds that had passed between his answer and when she'd asked the question made her doubt the statement. He didn't even sit like the Cooper Mead she knew, all slumped over, with none of the cocky self-assurance that made him the force to be reckoned with that he usually was.

Lainey plucked her phone off the coffee table and dialed.

The phone rang three times, four, five.

"Oh, you'd better pick up, you little—"

"Look, if you're calling to yell at me more about the bar, I'm—"

"What the hell happened to Coop?"

Brett's sigh whooshed through her earpiece. "Geez, Lainey. If you're going to date the guy, the least you can do is tune into the games. He was a hero tonight! Seriously, he dove—I'm talking full-on Superman—when Mack got caught out of his net and blocked this puck with his head in the dying seconds of the game and saved us from OT and possible elimination and—"

"He took a puck to the head?" Lainey reached over with her free hand, inspecting Cooper's hairline for a contusion, as he half-heartedly batted at her arm like he was shooing away a bothersome fly.

"Just the helmet. It was so awesome. The replay is all over the news."

"Was he acting weird at all on the plane today?"

"Nah. We watched some *Game of Thrones* on the flight. Said he had a bit of a headache, but other than that he seemed good. Why?"

"It's…" Lainey was on the verge of telling him, but caught herself short. Brett had proven she couldn't trust him, and even if she *did* trust him, her stupid brother wasn't known for his discretion. And if she was wrong… "I'm sure it's nothing. I'll call you later, okay?"

"Sure." There was a pause. "I'm glad you're still talking to me. Catch you later."

Lainey dropped the phone on the couch as she knelt in front of Coop.

"Cooper? I need you to look at me, okay?"

He turned his face toward her, but it was like he was staring through her, not at her.

"Cooper?"

He squeezed his eyes shut for a second before opening them again, and this time, Lainey felt the connection when he looked at her. His pupils didn't look wildly different in size.

"I'm fine. I'm… I got a headache on the plane. I'll be okay if I lie down."

"I'm going to call the hospital. You might have a concussion."

The word sobered him instantly. "I'm fine. No hospitals."

"You're not fine."

"Lainey, I played great tonight. We won because of me. The team needs me. If you call the doctor, my season's over. And I'm fine. Honestly. I'm tired is all." He sounded more like himself, but his words still seemed a bit slower than normal.

"What's your agent's name?"

"I fired that guy."

"What's his name, Cooper?"

"Gared Jolden." Coop's face screwed up with concentration. "No. Jared. Jared Golden." He overenunciated each syllable.

"Give me your phone."

Cooper fumbled with his suit jacket until he managed to produce his iPhone.

Lainey snatched it. "What's the passcode?"

"Huh?"

She held it out to him. "Punch in the passcode."

He punched in the number one four times in a row. When the screen unlocked, Lainey felt a wave of relief wash over her. He'd gotten the password on the first try. It might be simple—another consequence of his dyslexia, no doubt—but he'd remembered it, and she hoped that was a good sign, because she needed one right now, to keep her moving through the worry.

He looked up at her with puppy-dog eyes. "You're not gonna erase the video, are you?"

"What?"

"The video you made me. I didn't show it to anyone, Lainey, I swear. I would never do that. Please don't erase it, okay?"

"I won't erase it as long as you promise you'll stay here on the couch while I make this call, okay?" She scrolled through his contact list until she got to "J" and hit the phone icon.

"I won't go anywhere," Cooper promised solemnly as the call connected.

"I knew you'd come crawling back. And I'm willing to forgive you, Mead, because you were a fucking warrior out there tonight! My phone's been ringing off the hook, dude. PWR Athletics is kicking themselves that they let you go. They've called twice but I haven't answered yet. They're not only going to have to beg, they're going to have to pony up so much fucking bank that—"

"This isn't Cooper."

"Then who the fuck am I talking to?"

"It's Lainey Harper."

"The chick who scored on her own net. Yeah, I heard of you. I told Mead to dump your ass, but—"

"I think Cooper's got a concussion."

As it had with Cooper, the "C" bomb detonated with a cloud of utter silence.

Then, after a moment, Jared asked, "Who else knows about this?"

"No one, but I think he needs to go to the hospital."

"No! Nobody hears about this unless I okay it. This kind of thing can end a career, not just a season. Everybody's on edge about this shit right now. Are you with him?"

"Yeah. We're at his place, but—"

"Stay there. I'll send over a doctor. Do not answer the phone unless it's me, you got it?"

"I think—"

"Don't think. Just do what I tell you. When the doctor gets there, you need to get him up to the penthouse without any questions from the doorman, got it?"

She chafed at the order, but a quick glance at Cooper and his rumpled suit, the fear in his eyes when she'd mentioned the hospital, made her swallow her graphic suggestion of where Jared Golden could shove his attitude. She huffed instead. "This guy you're sending has a real medical degree, right? From an accredited school?"

"He's real. A Harvard grad. I know you're worried about Cooper, but this is a critical time in his career. We are in code red damage control right now. His performance tonight rejuvenated his stock. If he signs with me again, we could get PWR back."

Her hand squeezed the phone, trying to become a fist. "He might have brain damage, and you're making this all about money!"

"Lainey…it is Lainey, isn't it? I'm gonna let you in on the hard truth about professional sports—everything is about money."

It was a pleasure to hang up on the man.

Cooper seemed more lucid by the time Lainey had ushered the alleged Dr. Howard up to the suite.

He did some basic prodding and poking, checked Cooper's pupils with the flashlight on his goddamn key ring, asked a bunch of useless questions and declared that number sixteen was cleared to play before making a quick exit.

Lainey still wanted to take him to a real hospital, but Cooper insisted he was fine, and he seemed more like himself after he'd undressed and crawled into bed, assuring her that sleep was all he needed.

Lainey spent the rest of the night wide-awake, monitoring him for all the signs and symptoms of concussions that she'd found on the internet.

LAINEY HAD NO idea when she'd fallen asleep, but Cooper was gone when she woke up.

She winced at the kink in her neck, massaging it as she searched the bedding for her phone. She finally found it on the floor, and the screen informed her it was almost half past noon. She tried Cooper's phone, but the call went straight to voice mail.

She took a shower, made herself some toast and coffee, tried to distract herself with TV and gossip blogs, but nothing helped. She was acutely aware of every minute that ticked by until she heard Cooper's key in the lock, an hour and twenty-seven minutes later.

The sound was her cue.

She flicked the television off. And with a deep breath, she stood, squared her shoulders and prepared for battle.

"Hey." The word was noncommittal, but Lainey heard the faint note of surprise in Cooper's voice. He hadn't expected her to stay.

"You were gone when I woke up." It was an inane thing to say. Obvious. But Lainey couldn't bring herself to go with the stereotypically trite, "Where the hell have you been?" Especially since she knew the answer. He'd gone to the only place a hockey player one day away from the biggest game of his career would go.

"I went to practice. Reviewed some game tape. Had an easy skate."

She pushed down a scream so her voice would be level. "Are you sure that's a good idea?"

"It was fine. I feel fine." Cooper shot her a reassuring smile that didn't reach his eyes. "I hurt my brain, Lainey. Not something important, like a knee or a shoulder."

"Don't." The word cracked like a whip, and the dam of polite formality sprang a leak.

"It was a joke." His tone held the promise of bite, like a muzzled dog.

"Well, it wasn't funny. Don't put yourself down like that. You're not stupid. You have dyslexia."

"People treat you the same either way, so what's the difference?"

Lainey took a desperate step toward him. "You're worried about being stupid? Stupid is putting your health at risk for a game! A game that takes everything from you and gives nothing back."

"You don't get it, do you? This is what I'm good at, Lainey. Hockey. That's it. And once it's gone, I have nothing left." He dragged a hand through his hair. "I can't do what other retired hockey players do. I can't be a commentator or an analyst, because I can't read fast enough to keep up with the teleprompter. My future has 'washed-up has-been' written all over it."

"That's not true!"

"It is true." His voice was frighteningly matter-of-fact. "I know you think hockey ruined your life, but it saved mine. It saved me from feeling like an idiot. It saved me from being bullied. It gave me a future when school couldn't. And I can't believe you're so selfish that you want me to give it up, because you did."

Her eyes narrowed at the attack. "This has nothing to do with me."

"I'm closer to winning a championship than I've ever been in my career, and sponsors have dropped me anyway! That's what being an athlete is—your fate can change in an instant."

"You think I don't know that?" she cried. "Me?"

"Then you understand that I need to play tomorrow."

"Even if it means you can never play again?"

Cooper shook his head with a dismissive scoff. "Stop being melodramatic. It's one game, Lainey. Nothing's going to happen."

"That's exactly what you thought before that puck hit you."

She saw him disengage, retreat inside. The subtle shift from offense to defense as he pulled back from her.

"Cooper, listen to me." She held up her right forearm, so he could see her scar. "You've seen how much my wrist still affects my life. We're talking about your brain. One rogue puck, one bad hit—hell, one good hit—and forget not being able to play again, you might never walk again! You could lose your ability to speak, or to feed yourself. You need to find out how bad it is, and you need to give yourself time to heal. Please, I'm begging you. Get this looked at."

"I did. The doc said I'm fine."

"You know damn well that I mean by a doctor in a real hospital with equipment that's more high-tech than a key-chain flashlight." He was still standing in the same spot, but he was farther away than ever, and his distance frustrated her. "If you're so confident in his diagnosis, why don't you call the team doctors? Let them clear you instead of some guy being paid off by that scumbag Golden to make sketchy house calls in the middle of the night."

"Why do you even care?" The earnestness of the question was a slap in the face. The fact that he could ask her that, the fact that he didn't know.

"Why do I care? Cooper, I'm in love with you." Lainey's stomach dropped with that exhilarating free fall of roller coasters and big declarations. She was in love with Cooper Mead. She placed a hand on his forearm, eyes pleading. "And I'm asking you, if you care about me at all, not to play until you've been cleared."

"Oh, you love me now?" he jeered, shaking off her grip, and Lainey's bubble of pure, emotional honesty burst at the sharp sting of his words. "I'm not willing to give up everything for our 'magical' future, so now you love me?"

"What the hell is that supposed to mean?"

"It means *what* future, Lainey? You think I gave you those tickets so you could sell the bar? So you could leave? I gave them to you because I wanted you there, at the most important moment of my life. You've been trying to get out of here since the day we met. So focused on your plan. Sell the bar. Go hide out in your fancy hotel rooms. All you've wanted was to get your life back on track. But you've made it so there's no room for me in that life unless I give up my dream."

Lainey steeled her spine as he continued the unrelenting attack. "Now you're playing dirty. I didn't ask you to give up hockey to come with me."

"You didn't ask me anything. You've never considered me at all while making your decisions."

Her chin quivered, but she wrestled the sadness,

stayed in control. She'd known from that first night that Cooper was temporary. That they would never make it long-term. "If that's the way you feel, then maybe I should go."

Cooper's nod was like a dagger in her heart. "Yeah, maybe that's for the best."

And that was what Lainey told herself as she pulled the door shut behind her and headed for the elevator. That it was for the best.

18

"YOU HAVE MY TICKETS?"

Lainey stared at the man across from her. Allan Bashir was like a genie in a business suit, set to grant her wish with the stroke of his pen on the contract that sat on the desk between them. She held up the tickets in her hand.

The ones Cooper had given her, the ones that had represented so much more to him than a couple of seats in a packed arena. But she'd been too stupid to see it. Too scared to understand the meaning behind the gesture.

"Then I guess we have a deal, Ms. Harper." He signed his name with fluid precision before he spun the contract on the desk and pushed it toward Lainey, holding the expensive pen in her direction.

What the hell was she doing?

She'd told Cooper she loved him, but as soon as things got uncomfortable, she'd started running away. Like he'd said, there was no room for him in the life she led, traveling around from hotel room to hotel room. But if she stayed...

The thought didn't scare her anymore. Because somehow, over the last few months, it wasn't her dad's bar anymore. The Drunken Sportsman had become hers.

It had snuck into her being, and now it was hard to imagine her life without Aggie's frank observations, or Darius's snarky teasing or Brett's sibling loyalty, or Cooper's...everything.

She didn't want to imagine her life without Cooper.

Jeannie elbowed her, but instead of taking the pen, Lainey jumped to her feet. "My bar's not for sale."

Twin looks of disbelief greeted her sudden announcement.

"I'm sorry, Mr. Bashir. Your offer is more than fair. But my situation has changed."

"I'm afraid I don't understand."

Lainey shook her head, trying to figure out exactly what she meant. "I don't understand, either. When Mar— when my father left me the Sportsman, all I wanted was to sell it and get back to my life.

"I never thought I'd come to care about the people who work there. Or that I'd reconcile with my little brother or meet the guy who makes me want to face my past and overcome my fears."

Lainey shrugged. "But it happened. And now the bar kind of feels like...home." Admitting it aloud brought a warmth to her chest, a sense of belonging that had been missing for a long time.

"Family matters are often complicated."

Bashir's words blindsided her, stung the back of her eyes.

Family.

It was something she'd thought she'd lost when her dad walked out, when the car crash stole her mom too soon. But now she'd been given a second chance, and she'd be damned if she was going to give it up without a fight. She had to act fast.

"I have to go. I'm so sorry I wasted your time."

She hurried through the lobby of Mr. Bashir's gleaming office building, not slowing down until she found herself outside in the warm Portland evening.

There was a cab waiting on the corner, so she abandoned her Uber plan and crawled into the waiting vehicle.

"Can you take me to the Portland Dome, please?"

The cabbie complied, and Lainey mentally reviewed her to-do list.

She had a ride to the game.

She had tickets to the game.

There was only one thing left.

"I know it's in here somewhere." Lainey rifled through her purse until she found a creased business card in its depths and punched the numbers into her phone, bouncing her knee as she waited for the call to connect. "Pick up, pick up…"

"Hello?"

"Holly. Hi. It's Lainey Harper. I don't know if you remember me but—"

"Of course. What can I do for you, Lainey?"

"I was hoping you could help me out with something…"

THIS WAS IT—the biggest game of his career. As Cooper stood on the blue line looking up at the thousands of hockey fans standing, hands on hearts, as the final notes of the American national anthem played, he tried to absorb the moment. This was huge. Game seven of the championship series. Tonight, he could be part of sports history, have his name engraved on the trophy he'd coveted since the first time he'd strapped on a pair of skates. But as he stood there, beside his teammates, moments away from the puck drop, Cooper could only think of Lainey.

She wanted a future with him, had put herself out there to tell him that, and he'd been so afraid to admit to himself he wanted the same thing that he'd actually told her that hockey was the most important part of his life.

It had been, but it wasn't anymore, he realized. Lots of guys in the league did the long-distance thing so their kids had a stable home and weren't being jerked out of school and away from their friends with every trade. Surely two childless people with the means to buy airplane tickets could make a go of it.

As the lights in the arena came up, the players moved into position.

And Cooper made his choice.

He was at the box in four long strides.

"Sillinger."

"Dude, what are you doing over here? The game's about to start."

"I know." Coop reached over the boards and unlatched the gate. "You'd better get out there before the ref blows the whistle."

"But I—"

"I'm giving you your shot—go show these guys what you're made of. Go!"

The look of awe on Sillinger's face was priceless. "Thanks, Coop. I won't let you down."

Brett scrambled off the bench, shoving past Cooper and skating toward the Storm's side of the face-off circle, just in time for the puck drop.

Eric won the face-off cleanly, and slapped the puck

back to Brett…who bobbled it, and had to skate all the way back to the blue line to retrieve it before he finally passed it up the wing to Luke.

"Mead! What the hell's going on? Why is Sillinger out there?"

"I've got a concussion."

Taggert swore. "And you figured now was the best time to tell me?"

"It was the only time to tell you, Coach. Because I didn't realize how messed up I was until a few minutes ago."

"Shit, Mead. You need me to get the doc out here?"

Cooper shook his head. "Actually, I think I'm gonna be okay."

Three periods later, Cooper worried that he'd spoken too soon.

They were up 2-1, but Wisconsin was hitting them with heavy pressure, and the majority of the third period had taken place in the Storm's end of the rink.

When one of the Blades' forwards got the puck and swung out wide, beating Sillinger on the outside, Cooper thought they were in trouble. But instead of freaking out, Brett regrouped and executed a textbook poke-check to steal the puck back. He lobbed an incredible pass up the left side to Cubs, who was all alone as he buried one of his legendary wrist shots in the back of the net to give the Storm a commanding 3-1 lead with a minute left in the third.

The bench erupted with cheers.

"Holy shit!" Fourth-line defenseman Doug Kowal-chuk punched Cooper in the shoulder pad out of sheer excitement. "Did you see that pass? The rookie is on fire tonight!"

"Yeah, he is," Coop agreed, "so let's show him some respect and call him by his name. He's not a rookie anymore."

He'd spent the entire game worried that he wouldn't feel like part of the team if he wasn't out there, but in that moment, Cooper was pretty sure he couldn't have been prouder if he'd made the play himself.

When the buzzer finally sounded after the longest sixty seconds of Cooper's life, the Portland Dome exploded in cheers and Cooper joined his team as they scrambled over the boards and flooded onto the ice.

19

LAINEY FOLLOWED CLOSELY behind Holly and her cameraman, Jay, as they headed down the corridor that led to the ice, flashing the Women's Sport Network press pass Holly had given her at the appropriate checkpoints until they were finally allowed out onto the rink. She hesitated for a moment before she stepped through the gate, inhaling that unique mix of cold and rubber and sweat. The scent of hockey. It had been a long time.

This was it. The moment she'd avoided for so long. Ice level, where all her bad memories lived. But as she stood there, surrounded by people who were still able to play the game she loved, she realized something.

When her father hurt her, she'd cut him with a couple of official name-change documents.

When hockey hurt her, she'd cut it out of her life just as swiftly.

But out on that ice were two people who were worth the risk of getting hurt again.

With a deep breath, Lainey stood up to her deepest fears and stepped onto the ice.

It was easier than she'd thought it would be.

"We're going to go do some interviews," Holly yelled over the din of the cheering crowd and the booming baseline of "We Are the Champions," as it blared throughout the arena. "You got it from here?"

Lainey nodded, tearing her eyes from the jubilant crowd and the navy, white and teal confetti that spilled from the rafters. Thanks to the press pass, she'd gained a head start, but they'd be ushering the players' families down to the ice to join in the celebration and then it would be near impossible to find—

"Lainey?" Brett skated toward her so fast that the blades of his skates sprayed snow on her boots when he stopped in front of her. "Lainey! You're here! Did you see how much ice time I got? And my assist on Cubs's goal? Nobody called me 'Rookie' during the whole game! This is the best night of my life!"

Lainey couldn't help but smile at his enthusiasm. He was practically bouncing, he was so excited. She'd always thought this moment would make her jealous, but it was a different emotion winding its way through her chest now. It was pride.

She'd spent so much time cutting hockey out of her life, but it was a part of her. A part of her family.

It took all her meager acting abilities to wipe the smile from her face before she heaved a fake sigh and held her arms out.

Her abrupt change in demeanor subdued Brett, and he shoved sweaty dark curls off his forehead. "What?"

"I owe you a hug, don't I?"

She hadn't thought his grin could get any bigger, but

not even his scraggly playoff beard could hide the joy on his face.

He reeked of the hot-sour stench of hockey equipment as he wrapped his arms around her waist and swung her in a circle. Beneath the roar of the crowd and the interviews and the music, Brett spoke softly in her ear. "Thanks for coming, Elaine."

It ranked among the top five hugs of her life.

He set her down and she tried to wipe the tear from her cheek before he noticed.

"Are you crying?"

It didn't work.

"I can't help it, okay?" Lainey crossed her arms. "I'm so happy you can finally shave that ridiculous excuse for a beard."

Brett chuckled at the jibe, but it was far too somber for a man who'd just played an integral role in securing a national championship. "Hey, what I said before? About you being like Dad? You're not."

She waved away the apology. "Go. Take your victory lap. Celebrate with your team. We can talk that stuff out later. Right now, you need to enjoy the moment. You did good tonight."

The warm glow in the pit of her stomach dissipated as she watched Brett skate away, back to the thick of the celebration. Because now was the moment of truth.

Cooper was standing with his back to her, decked out in full Storm gear, his last name and the number sixteen gleaming against the navy jersey, exchanging a word and a bro hug with his team captain, and Lainey didn't think she'd ever been more in danger of puking in her entire life. Even waiting to find out if she'd made the national team paled in comparison to this. She walked toward him slowly, not because she was worried about falling, but, she realized, lips twisting at the irony, because she'd already fallen.

She'd fallen hard for the infuriating, sexy man who was a mere ten feet from her now. Luke noticed her as she stopped to wipe her sweaty hands on her jeans and compose herself.

Their eyes met for a moment before Luke tipped his chin in her direction, causing Cooper to glance over his shoulder. There was a jolt in her chest as they stared at each other, as if her nervous system had short-circuited, and her heartbeat went from zero to tachycardia in the space of a second.

Cooper turned and pushed off his back blade in one fluid motion. Despite the revelry in the arena, all she could hear was the scrape of his skates as he stopped in front of her. He was always tall and broad, but in full equipment, he was massive. She did her best to focus on his eyes. They were wary, but they were familiar, and she clung to that as she forced herself to say what she'd come here to say.

"I forgot."

She'd surprised him. She knew him well enough to recognize the almost imperceptible twitch of his eyebrow, which was his tell.

"Forgot what?"

"How the ice smells. It's been a long time. I missed it, but it doesn't hurt like I thought it would." Saying it out loud made Lainey realize how true it was. She might have ended her hockey career on a low note, but there were good memories here on the blue line, too. Playing hockey wasn't her future. But maybe, just maybe, the man in front of her could be. The thought gave her the courage to say, "I don't miss it like I missed you."

"I didn't think you'd come."

She shrugged. "Well, after I decided not to sell the bar, I had these hockey tickets that I figured shouldn't go to waste."

Cooper's eyes widened at the announcement. "You're staying?"

"It turns out that Portland has some redeeming qualities after all. Figured I might stick around and see what it has to offer."

"Have you told Brett?"

"I wanted to tell you first. I thought it might be a good way to show you that I've made room for you in my life. And I know, after everything, you might not believe this, but I'm so sorry they wouldn't let you play, Cooper. I know how important this game was to you. To your career."

"*You're* important to me," he countered. "And when I took the ice tonight, I could hear you in my head, talking about the future, and I decided you were right. The risk wasn't worth it. So I benched myself. Because if I'm going to keep up with you and your smart mouth, I'm going to need my brain to be functioning on all cylinders. That's the price of falling in love with the smartest, hottest, toughest woman I've ever met, and...are you crying?"

"Maybe." She swiped at the stupid tears on her stupid cheek. "And people say that *I'm* the one who knows how to fuck up a moment."

"Oh, I'll give you a moment." Cooper grabbed her and hoisted her up so high that when she wrapped her legs around his waist and her arms around his neck, he was the one who had to look up at her. And when Lainey lowered her mouth to his, their kiss held the promise of a lifetime of moments to come.

* * * * *

If you loved this book, check out
Taryn Leigh Taylor's other hot romances:

KISS AND MAKEUP
PLAYING TO WIN

Available now from Harlequin Blaze!

COMING NEXT MONTH FROM

HARLEQUIN™ Blaze®

Available May 23, 2017

#943 ONE NIGHT WITH A SEAL (anthology)
Uniformly Hot!
by Tawny Weber and Beth Andrews
What could be sexier than twin Navy SEAL brothers searching for their happily-ever-afters? Read the ultimate Uniformly Hot! Blaze—two stories in one!

#944 OFF LIMITS MARINE
by Kate Hoffmann
After her husband died, Annie Foster Jennings swore she'd never marry another military man. But if anyone can change her mind, it's sweet, sexy pilot Gabe Pendleton.

#945 EASY RIDE
by Suzanne Ruby
Aspiring reporter Kirby Montgomery goes undercover at an exclusive club. But when she falls for the subject of her story, Adam Drake—nickname Easy Ride—all bets are off.

#946 NOTORIOUS
by Vicki Lewis Thompson
When rancher Noah Garfield spots Keely Branscom in Sin City, he decides it's his duty to reform the bad girl from his past. Which should be easy...unless Keely tempts him with her wild ways!

HBCNM0517

Get 2 Free Books,
<u>Plus</u> 2 Free Gifts—
just for trying the Reader Service!

HDI7

"The Bennett brothers are coming home?"

A thrill of delight shot through Vivian Harris at the
news.

"Yep, Xander and Zane should be here—" Mike
looked at his watch and grinned "—within the hour."

"Both of them?" At her brother's scowl, Vivian made
a show of sweeping her long blond bangs away from her
face and giving him a wide-eyed look of concern. "Are
you sure Little Creek can handle an invasion by the Bad
Boy Bennetts?"

"Probably not," Mike replied with a laugh. "Luckily
they're only here for ten days. Other than breaking a few
hearts, I don't think they can do much damage with so
little time."

"Last time they were only home a week and they got
into a huge bar fight after you challenged them to see

who could drink the most shots. They broke the table at the diner arm wrestling, and if rumor is correct, they were seen streaking down Main Street at three in the morning as part of some insane decathlon." Oh, how she'd wept over missing that sight.

"Nah, the streaking was just a rumor. But the rest are true." Mike's grin widened. "I'm going to have to do some serious thinking if I'm going to top all of those challenges."

Vivian had a few challenges she wouldn't mind offering Zane. Talk about a dream worth living—if only for ten days.

Her fingers tapping a beat on the scarred surface of the bakery counter, Vivian gave herself a minute to delve into her favorite fantasy. The one that starred her and Zane Bennett covered in nothing but chocolate frosting and a few tempting dollops of whipped cream.

Maybe it was time to try out a few of her dreams on something other than her bakery business. After all, if she could make a glistening penis-shaped cake worthy of oohs and ahhs, how hard could it be to get her hands on Zane Bennett's real one?

Vivian flashed a wicked smile.

Hopefully, once she got her hands on it, it'd be very, very hard.

Don't miss
ONE NIGHT WITH A SEAL
by Tawny Weber and Beth Andrews.

Available June 2017 wherever
Harlequin Blaze books and ebooks are sold.

www.Harlequin.com

Turn your love of reading into rewards you'll love with
Harlequin My Rewards